Inconvenient Pipeline

Geoff Strong

Geoff Strong

Story Illustrations: Mary Lynn French and Jenessa Strong
Cover Art: Laura Timmermans

Illustrations: Mary Lynn French and Jenessa Strong
Cover Art: Laura Timmermans

Published: Climate Crisis Publications

Library and Archives Canada Cataloguing in Publication
Strong, G. S. (Geoffrey Stuart), 1945-, author
Inconvenient Pipeline / Geoff Strong.

Issued in print and electronic formats.
ISBN 978-0-9952883-2-4 (softcover)
ISBN 978-0-9952883-3-1 (ebook)

KEYWORDS: pipeline, oil spills, big oil, climate change, corporate greed, eminent domain, energy, environmental justice, fossil fuels, property rights, oil sands, tanker disaster, indigenous respect.

Contact Geoff Strong: www.climatecrisis2020.ca

Geoff Strong

Disclaimer and Motivation

This is a work of fiction, and all events and characters portrayed are fictional. Some events draw upon actual happenings that have occurred in other locations and times. For example, the oil tanker break-up and major oil spill described in Chapter 22 has not happened, but it is based on a similar oil spill disaster caused in 1970 by the tanker *SS Arrow*, which went aground in Chedabucto Bay NS, contaminating 300 kilometres of coastline after it broke in half and sank. Beaches remain spoiled on Chedabucto Bay shorelines 50 years later in 2020. The Arrow disaster helped inspire this novel, because the author played a role during the clean-up operation as the on-site weather forecaster. Archival Arrow photos are reproduced on p. 127-128.

The *Arrow* contained 10 million litres of Bunker-C oil, and attempts to clean up the spill were futile. While oil spills are often under-estimated to avoid negative publicity, clean-up success is over-estimated, and is rarely even 10% successful on water. Much of the *Arrow* oil was left to wash away, but it clung to beaches, plants and wildlife. Attempts were still being made to pump out a remaining 20,000 litres of oil from the *Arrow* in 2015, so that this disaster justifies concerns for increased tanker traffic in the Strait of Georgia after oil exits the pipeline. For many British Columbians, new pipelines to the coast represent more potential problems than just being *inconvenient*.

The Covid-19 global health crisis in 2020 should remind us that there cannot be a healthy economy without a healthy environment and climate. A First Nations saying worth remembering is: *We do not inherit the Earth from our ancestors … We borrow it from our children and grandchildren.* We must look after our atmosphere, land, and ocean for them.

Dedication

This novel is dedicated to that brilliant Swedish teenage activist, Greta Thunberg, who has independently motivated millions of youth around the world to protest the lack of government actions on the climate crisis; to First Nations people in Canada, who have launched courageous battles, legal and otherwise, against financial powers and careless environmental practices of petroleum corporations; and to my future great-grandchildren, the first of whom came into this damaged world in 2019. My hope is that their generation will do a better job of caring for the environment and climate than we have done. Last but not least, to my dogs Buddy and Denny, always by my side and who safeguard my sanity when life gets tough.

Testimonials

Inconvenient Pipeline is a charming novel with an environmental message that becomes all the more compelling, precisely because it is interwoven with such a heart-warming story. A great read for all ages.

This well-crafted story centres on the Nicholson family (Eric, a climate scientist at UVan, Carol, a meteorologist with Environment Canada, Julia going into grade 10 and John going into grade 6). With a camper trailer and canoe, they embark on a fishing holiday near Merritt, British Columbia. Because they are sociable and curious, they meet and interact with a large cast of characters during their two-week sojourn in a pristine wilderness on the edge of a pipeline. The story is suspenseful, and the plot takes unexpected and coincidental twists and turns that surprise and occasionally bring tears to the eye.

Without preaching and unnecessary polemics, the author broaches some of the real-life moral and ethical implications of environmental issues, particularly pipelines, oil spills and the first nations communities they impact. The multiple sub-plots and themes are skillfully interwoven to create a story that is both fascinating, realistic and endearing.

Highly recommended for all ages, but especially for teens, who will relate to the central characters.

Prof. E.P. Lozowski
Atmospheric Scientist Emeritus, University of Alberta, Edmonton

I commend you for writing a story that is sorely needed. I really liked the adventures of the Nicholson family, the people they meet, and their camping and canoeing adventures. It was a pleasure to read and I'm so glad you sent it.

Bette Kosmolak
Author, 02 April 2020

Inconvenient Pipeline tells the story of an eco-aware family that stumbles upon a dangerous pipeline oil spill. The thematic fabric of the novel is a tight weave of environmental, economic, social, and health issues as seen through the heads and hearts of the various effected characters, including pipeline company employees, a First Nations band, and other residents of a British Columbia rural community. Particularly suitable for young readers, this book makes a case for a universal redesigning of our energy sources, and it does so with intelligence and urgency.

Jonathan Churcher
Wordsmith and Singer/Songwriter

The subject is interesting and there are some neat twists to the story that keeps one reading; a pretty good read.

Pat Fraser
(author, *The Mystery Behind the Shaman's Call*)

A charming portrayal of a family coming to grips with 21st century environmental destruction and intrigue. With just the right balance between authoritative science and compelling storytelling, this is a book the entire family can enjoy together.

Garth Mihalcheon
Management Consultant

Inconvenient Pipeline *delivers information about climate change, pollution and land governance and consent issues in a clear way that makes understanding complex issues such as these easy. However, environmental issues are not the only ones touched upon in "Inconvenient Pipeline" as the book discusses mental health issues, ethical questions and indigenous culture. The book also goes to great length in describing the geography of British Columbia, and encourages a sense of adventure. Overall, Inconvenient Pipeline is an exciting piece of fiction for young people interested in environmental issues.*

Katia Bannister
Youth Climate Activist

***

Acknowledgements

I am grateful to my wife Phyllis, who endures the many hours I spend on research, writing, and presentations. She sits through my church talks on international aid (on behalf of the Anglican Church of Canada), and my endless talks to secular groups on global warming impacts. She reads my many writings to give helpful feedback. For example, for a short story I wrote with the title *Wildfire Trap*, Phyllis pointed out that *Trapped by Wildfires* would enliven the title, and as always, she was right. Phyllis is my biggest supporter and harshest critic, and while she may not understand much of the science, I have learned to value her input.

Thanks go to graphics artists, Mary Lynn French, whose enthusiasm caused her to bombard me with many line drawings, including most of those appearing in this novel; Laura Timmermans, who completed the cover in water colours; to my granddaughter, Jenessa Strong, who helped during the final completion of this novel by drawing the 'treasure map', and granddaughter Isabelle Gronning and her dad Dave, who helped in a final pinch (to what I leave readers to guess).

I also acknowledge several helpful reviewers who provided the early testimonials on the preceding pages: Dr Edward Lozowski, an excellent scientist (who also supervised both my graduate theses many years ago); authors Bette Kosmolak and Pat Fraser; singer/songwriter Jonathan Churcher; consultant Garth Mihalcheon; and most important, youth climate activist Katia Bannister, a local version of Greta Thunberg. Many of their comments were valuable in the final editing process.

***

Story Setting

The primary setting for this story is in the immediate vicinity of the city of Merritt (centre of map) in the Nicola valley of south-central BC. The older 1950s pipeline approximately follows the Coquihalla Highway (#5) bolded on the map.

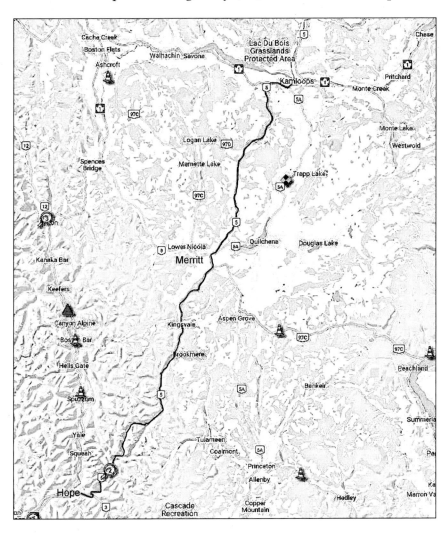

Map of south-central BC with Coquihalla Highway (#5) which is bolded from Hope to Merritt to Kamloops.

Contents

Copyright ii

Disclaimer and Justification.. iii

Dedication iv

Testimonials v

Acknowledgements viii

Story Setting...ix

Contents...xi

Introduction xiii

1. Julia Averts an Oil Tanker Disaster.............................1

2. Greenhouse Gases are not Pollutants........................6

3. The Nicholson Family 12

4. Summer Holiday 15

5. Oil Spill and Mystery Box.......................................18

6. Julia Discovers Oil Leak Source 26

7. Mystery Dog 32

8. The Horsekey Ranch...39

9. Confession...43

10. Mystery Treasure Restored....................................47

11. A Better Deal for Ranchers....................................50

12. The Young Mystery Drifter.....................................53

13. Awards and Rewards 61

14. The Prodigal Son 67

15. Nicholsons go Riding 72

16. Trouble at Englishmen Lake....................................76

17. Career Decision for Tom 82

18. Corporate Deception 85

19. Investigation of Pipeline Break 90

20. Potlatch 98

21. First Nations Western Conference 109

22. Oil Tanker Disaster 112

23. Disaster Aftermath..123
24. Epilogue..127

Appendix - Main Characters.....................................130
Abbreviations and Definitions.................................132
Author Biographical Sketch.....................................133
If you enjoyed this novel...135

Introduction

After writing the first four chapters of this novel, Phyllis and I were poking around a tidy little thrift shop in Courtenay, BC when I came across the small box pictured below. The symbols on its cover, a rearing horse and a key intrigued me. Without thinking how or why, I decided that it would command a focus in the novel, and so it captures attention in the first half. I still have not determined the mystery of the two symbols, but perhaps Julia was correct in connecting it to a ranch.

Mystery box that Julia finds near an oil spill. Photo by G. Strong.

This story is a prequel to an earlier account in this series, *Convenient Mistruths*, involving the same family members at various stages in their lives. Julia and John take lead roles and are 13 and 9 years old in this story.

Geoff Strong
Atmospheric/Climate Scientist and Novelist
28 April, 2020

Inconvenient Pipeline

1. Julia Averts an Oil Tanker Disaster

"Dad, oil is leaking from that tanker," Julia yelled.

Julia and her dad, Eric Nicholson, had launched their canoe at Vanier Park boat dock near the museum in Vancouver, and then paddled along the west shore of Stanley Park. They were trying out her new 13-foot Kodiak canoe on a warm Saturday in early May.

Her parents had given the canoe to Julia on her 13th birthday three months before. Julia was in Grade 8, the consummate tom-boy. She loved sports, including soccer, baseball, hockey, tennis, hiking in the wilderness, and playing with her dog, a Golden Retriever named Buddy, who was less than a year old. Julia excelled in her school work. Her favourite sport was canoeing, which her parents had been sharing with her since she was eight years old.

"Which tanker, Julia?" her dad asked, for there were three tanker ships visible ahead on Burrard Inlet.

"The red one on the right–there appears to be oil pouring off the stern."

"Yes, I see it now. But no one on board seems concerned about it. They haven't noticed the leak yet. We need to call Harbour Security people so they can warn the tanker."

Julia's favourite sport was canoeing.

Eric and Julia knew that a large oil spill near Vancouver had the potential to spoil water activities and fishing for years to come. The nearby sandy beach had hundreds of sun-seekers staked out all along it. Even though it was only early May, the warm weather brought thousands of people out to Stanley Park.

They paddled closer to shore, and Eric pulled his cell phone out of a waterproof pouch and called Security and Emergency Management at Harbour Security. They had not known of the leak, so after getting the details from Eric, they thanked him and got an investigation underway. Less than ten minutes later, as Julia and Eric took advantage of the beach for a break, they noticed a helicopter swooping out over Burrard Inlet headed straight for the tanker. The ship's crew had been informed and were working at stopping the oil coming off at the rear of the tanker.

They resumed their paddling, and Julia remarked, "I guess that's one reason many people oppose the proposed pipeline from Alberta? However, our teacher said that some First Nations bands favour the pipeline. Why is that, Dad?"

"The pipeline is an opportunity for some people, but is an *inconvenient pipeline* for others." As they headed south along the shore toward False Creek where they had launched a few hours earlier, Eric added, "The pipeline can entice some people to find a good-paying job while it is being built. Most of those jobs disappear once they complete the pipeline. After that, they need trained technical people to supervise, plan pipeline loads, and check for leaks. Few people have sufficient training for those jobs, so they bring in specialists from outside."

"So it would provide short-term gain with no long-term benefits?"

"Yes, although that job might lead to other opportunities. One of the biggest concerns for British Columbia is the risk of a tanker spill *after* the oil leaves the pipeline. We just observed a small example of that. And it's easy to imagine what would happen if a tanker collided with another ship or a rocky shoal, especially if combined with poor weather and nighttime shipping. Then goodbye to these beaches we're seeing along Stanley Park here, for both locals and tourists, not to mention the likelihood of the closure of fishing through much of the Strait of Georgia."

"Where can we see a pipeline?"

"The main Trans-Mountain pipeline runs into the Burnaby terminal, but it's underground. We can look it up on-line when we get home. However, the same pipeline runs by the town of

Merritt, which we can observe on our vacation in July. Remind me then."

***

Julia and her dad could not have known that the oil tanker leak that day was a prelude to what would happen four months later in September. An oil tanker would depart from the port of Burnaby after loading with heavy crude oil from the pipeline terminus. The Strait of Juan de Fuca would have gale force winds forecast by midnight, but they expected to be out over the open Pacific by then. Unfortunately, their expectation of a safe passage would not be realized because of the fickleness of nature and human technology.

***

After loading the canoe onto the rooftop carrier, Eric received a call back from Vancouver Port Authority.

"Hi Mr. Nicholson. I'm the community liaison officer at the Vancouver Port Authority, and I'm calling to thank you for reporting that leaking oil tanker. The problem is now corrected, but it could have caused a nasty oil spill if not for your prompt report."

"Oh, you need to speak with my 13-year-old daughter, Julia. She first noted the spill; I simply gave you the report." He handed the phone to Julia.

"Hello", said Julia.

After speaking with the liaison person for several minutes, Julia thanked her and shut off the phone.

"They're inviting our entire family to a special luncheon in

4

our honour next Friday; the lady will call you back later today with details."

"Why, that's wonderful, Julia! That will please your mother and John."

After arriving home, and while Julia was cleaning up their canoe equipment, Eric explained to Carol what had happened. "We are all invited to a special luncheon event. We have a sharp-eyed daughter who is sensitive to the environment."

"Yes, we are blessed with both of our kids," Carol replied.

***

2. Greenhouse Gases are not Pollutants

The following Friday, the Nicholsons were driving to the luncheon when Julia's brother, John spoke up.

"Why is the air so smoky blue, and the sun appears red, Dad?" John asked.

"That's very observant that you notice that, John. It's because of air pollution, and it's caused by many things, including smoke from factories in the city, exhausts from cars and trucks, and smoke from burning wood and trash. Today, it's because of forest fires in the mountains east of here, and the wind direction is bringing that smoke right down over Vancouver."

"It wasn't like this yesterday," countered John.

"No, because yesterday the wind was from the west, from out over the Strait of Georgia, but the wind changed direction overnight and now it's coming from the northeast, bringing smoke from the forest fires."

"Is it bad for us to breathe," asked John?

"It is today, that's for sure," replied Eric.

"We've been learning about air and water pollution in science this week," added Julia.

"So why is the air pollution bad for breathing?" asked John.

"My science teacher says the smoke has tiny particles of soot and ash in it, and when you breathe those in, they can cause all kinds of problems in your lungs, making it difficult to breathe at all," replied Julia.

"Is that why they call it air pollution?" asked John.

"That's right," added Eric, "and there are other kinds of

pollution, including water pollution and soil pollution, for example."

"I suppose if you drink polluted water, it can hurt your stomach, just like air pollution hurts your lungs."

Eric nodded.

John was undeterred from this conversation and continued, "What kinds of water pollution are there?"

"Water gets polluted if garbage gets into it, or certain chemicals, human or animal waste, or oil; many things can pollute water. That's why government has to protect our drinking water sources. Some pollution causes bacteria to grow, and when serious enough, those bacteria can kill humans. Other forms of pollution, like chemicals, or paints, or oil products in the water can poison us and kill us even quicker. We'll hear more about oil pollution at the luncheon today."

Carol interjected at this point with "When we go on holidays next month, let's all be observant about both air and water pollution."

John persisted, "I heard you and Mom talking about green gases. Are they pollutants too, Dad?"

"You mean greenhouse gases, John, and no, they are not pollutants, although many think so because they are produced by the same process, through the burning of fossil fuels, like gasoline, natural gas, coal, and even wood and paper. Forest fires also emit carbon dioxide."

"So, like carbon monoxide from cars?"

"Yes, but the difference is that carbon monoxide is a poisonous gas, a pollutant. The reason I say that most greenhouse gases are not pollutants or poisonous in negligible quantities, is because nature produces them, and they are essential in three ways. First, vegetation absorbs carbon dioxide, or CO_2 for short, from the atmosphere, and together with nutrients and water from the soil, plus the sun's heat, the plant grows!"

"So CO_2 helps provide food for us, right?"

"Yes, but just as important, while the plant takes in CO_2, it releases oxygen or O_2 back to the atmosphere, which humans and all animals need to breathe."

"You mean that carbon dioxide also provides oxygen for us to breathe?"

"Yes, and there is a third reason why *natural* amounts of CO_2 (and other greenhouse gases) are important - they help maintain the natural heat balance on Earth."

Eric realized that he was going too deep into the science for a nine-year-old. *But heck*, he thought, *John is a smart kid, and he's not afraid to ask questions if he loses the trail.*

"How do greenhouse gases do that, Dad?"

"Well, greenhouse gases have special properties at the tiny molecular level that allows them to absorb heat in the atmosphere, and then radiate that heat back to the Earth's surface. Other gases, like oxygen and nitrogen, don't have that capability."

"Oh, so these greenhouse gases are like mirrors?"

"No, but greenhouse gases like carbon dioxide act somewhat like a garden greenhouse, similar to Mr. Tilden's greenhouse next door to us. There, sunshine passes through the glass panels. When the sun's rays hit a solid dark object inside, like the soil, they're absorbed and create heat, which then warms the air inside the greenhouse. Heat is trapped inside and cannot pass back through the glass."

He paused while John thought about this.

"Mr. Tilden explained his greenhouse to me just like that."

"Good. In a similar way, sunshine heats the Earth. Then the Earth radiates some of this heat back to space. But greenhouse gases in the atmosphere, like water vapour, carbon dioxide, and methane, absorb some of that heat, and then radiate it back to Earth. This is similar to a garden greenhouse, and that's why we call them *greenhouse gases*. Okay?"

"Yeah, I think I understand that now, but why did you and Mom say that greenhouse gases are bad?"

Oh, oh, thought Eric, *now I've gone too far and I'm in trouble. But it's too late to stop now.*

"Well, since the Industrial Revolution started, humans have been burning more and more fossil fuels - far *too much*, in fact, and now we have too much greenhouse gases in the atmosphere, sending too much heat back to Earth. So the atmosphere and oceans are now being heated too much."

"I see. I think I get it now, Dad. So we need to stop burning fossil fuels, right?"

"Yes, we need to stop burning so much fuel like that. But it's not possible to stop it all at once, John. Think about it. We could not take our holiday in July if we didn't burn some gasoline and produce some greenhouse gases. That's why humans are developing energy from other sources, like the sun, wind, tides, and so on. None of these release pollutants or greenhouse gases. However, there are thousands of people whose jobs depend on producing those fossil fuels. They first need retraining for other trades."

"I see," said John, although he seemed a little puzzled now.

"Well, here we are at the Vancouver Port Authority, so let's find out where the luncheon is."

"Wow!" John remarked. "My sister is a hero for stopping that oil pollution."

They were formally welcomed to the luncheon in Julia's honour. The keynote speaker mentioned the proposed new pipeline, with increased tanker traffic, and the necessity for more diligence by people like Julia to be wary of possible oil pollution.

On their way home following the luncheon, Julia asked, "Dad, if we're burning too much fossil fuel, why are they planning to build another pipeline from Alberta to Vancouver? Won't we have more of those big oil tankers around then, and probably more tanker leaks like we saw last weekend? And, people burn that fuel somewhere else, putting more greenhouse gases into the atmosphere."

"You're right, and that's the same question that many people are asking, Julia, and there's no simple answer. Much will depend on how our First Nations people and bands react, since the pipeline must cross their traditional lands."

"We have a girl in my class from the Burrard Inlet Indian Band. She says the Canadian Petroleum Corporation have met with their band and have offered big paying jobs if the band signs some document saying they approve of the pipeline. Her dad is Chief of the Burrard Band, and he is against the pipeline, so there's been a big argument among band members about it."

"Oh, have they resolved the argument yet?"

"Yes, he convinced band members that jobs would only be

available while the pipeline is being built. Once it's built, the jobs might all disappear. And by the way, they don't call it the Burrard Indian Band anymore; they are the ... sail wa-tooth - how do you say it ..."

"The *tslay-wah-tooth* (Tsleil-Waututh) Nation. That's interesting. I wonder if the oil company is approaching all the bands in that way."

Carol interrupted with, "CBC interviewed some CEO from Canadian Petroleum in Calgary last evening, and he denied that either the oil companies or their pipeline company were doing anything like that. He claims it's a rumour started by various environmental activists."

"It will be interesting to see if there's any truth to the rumours. I wouldn't be surprised if it is true."

***

3. The Nicholson Family

Eric was a professor at the University of Vancouver (UVan), teaching climate science and carrying out climate research. He was also a contributing member of the Intergovernmental Panel on Climate Change (IPCC). His wife, Carol, was a professional meteorologist and a senior forecaster for Environment Canada in Vancouver. Both Julia and her kid brother John showed great interest in environmental issues, and Eric and Carol encouraged conversations on these.

Carol grew up on the west coast in Victoria, while Eric came from the Eastern Shore region of Nova Scotia. They met in Montreal in 1987 when she was completing forecast training, and he was in graduate studies at McGill University. They married in 1989 just before Eric started PhD studies at the University of Maryland. Eric went to Beijing in 1993 as a post-doctoral fellow. They returned to Canada in 1994 where he was offered the position at UVan by his former MSc supervisor. Julia was born the following February. She was just completing Grade 8.

John was nine, four years younger than his sister Julia, and was just finishing Grade 4. He was a typical boy for his age, and enjoyed team sports like baseball, soccer, and swimming. He liked school, but mainly for social interaction with his friends; and according to his teacher, he was prone to day-dreaming during classes. Most of all, he was excited about the upcoming summer holidays, wanting to try out his new fishing rod with his dad.

Eric smiled to himself as he recalled an incident from a few years earlier when he had picked John up from his Grade 1 class. John was strapped into his rear booster seat, and while stopped at a traffic light, Eric noticed him leaning back and looking out the rear window of their car. Eric asked him, "What are you looking at there, son?"

"Just the clouds," he replied.

"That's what your mom does; she studies clouds and weather."

After a few moments of silence, John said, "Hmm, maybe Mom should get a different job if all she does is look at clouds."

That's what your mom does. She studies clouds and weather.

The family now lived in suburban Vancouver, close to UVan, and they were all looking forward to getting away from the city in early July for a two-week vacation of camping, fishing, and canoeing in the British Columbia interior.

They had bought a new Toyota Highlander hybrid SUV for its carrying capacity and good fuel mileage, and had also purchased a small used travel trailer for the holiday. The plan was to take the 19-ft family canoe on this trip. Eric looked forward to spending some undistracted time with the family. Carol, who was an accomplished writer, planned to spend some of her time researching and writing on the Pacific Western pipeline. She was writing a book on how pipelines were impacting First Nations people in British Columbia.

Eric and Carol had long-term plans to take the family camping and canoeing in the Northwest Territories someday, but not before the kids were excellent canoeists and swimmers. So, this summer's holiday would be the first real test for that future adventure.

***

4. Summer Holiday

Julia and John arrived home after their last Friday of school before holidays. Julia had just completed Grade 8. She clapped her hands and yelled, "We're going on holidays! Whoo-hoo! I can't wait to go canoeing!"

"But Sis, we're going camping," spoke up John.

"Yes, both," replied his big sister. "And fishing, and seeing the stars at night that we can't see here in Vancouver because of the air and light pollution."

"Wow, I'm gonna catch the biggest fish ever!" John replied.

"Hold on you two," said their mom. "We have plenty to do and to pack before we can head out on the road Monday morning. So you two make sure you finish your chores, and get Buddy's things ready to go too - his bed, food, bowls, leashes. Meanwhile, there's the little matter of report cards; how did you do?"

"Oh Mom, you know we both did well in school. I heard you speaking with both our teachers. John-boy did excellent in Grade 4. His teacher told me this afternoon."

"Oh, and what about you?" joked their mother.

"Probably failed, unless... See for yourself!" she replied, passing over both report cards.

"Only As. Can't you do better than that?"

"Nope, that's as high as it gets," piped up John.

"Well, I guess your dad and I will have to be satisfied with that."

Both kids were keen about their school work; in fact, they

enjoyed school, and both were popular with their peers and teachers. Their reward was this summer trip into the British Columbia interior in July.

***

The Nicholson family headed out on Highway 1 eastward from Vancouver on the last day of June. They were pulling their small travel trailer with the family canoe strapped onto their Toyota. They had planned to stop for lunch in Hope. However, some 30 kilometers southwest of Hope, they had to detour off Highway 1 onto Highway 9 which led across the Fraser River to Agassiz, later crossing the river again into Hope.

Small travel trailer with the family canoe strapped onto their Toyota Highlander hybrid SUV.

During lunch, they learned that there had been a pipeline break during the construction of a new access road just west of Hope, spilling thousands of litres of oil. Because of the proximity of the Fraser River, closure of Highway 1 and an emergency cleanup was essential. In retrospect, they viewed this diversion as an ominous forewarning of what was to come in Merritt.

After lunch in Hope, they took the Coquihalla Highway, arriving in the town of Merritt during late-afternoon, in time to check into Claybanks RV Park right on the banks of the Coldwater River.

Eric had chosen slow, shallow, winding rivers with good trout fishing for their holiday. The Coldwater River south of the city of Merritt and the Nicola River to the northeast were both slow meandering rivers. They merged just west of the city. Merritt had excellent facilities and a clean campground on the banks of the Coldwater on the south side of town.

"When can we go fishing, Dad?" John asked as soon they had stopped.

"Well, if your mother agrees, perhaps you can fish right here after we have dinner."

"Do we need a license to fish, Dad," asked Julia?

"Your mother and I have licenses, but you kids get to fish free in British Columbia."

***

5. Oil Spill and Mystery Box

The next day after breakfast, Eric asked the kids, "Would you like to canoe up the Nicola River, maybe fish as we go?"

"Sure!" Julia and John answered in unison.

"Can I paddle," asked John?

"Yes, we'll take turns in the canoe. You remember our lessons from last year?"

"Two of us paddle and take turns," replied John.

"Right. Your mother wants to spend some time this morning on her book. So you two will paddle first, while I read for a while. We'll take our fishing rods and see if we can catch supper for us all," Eric said, winking at Carol.

"I'll catch one *thissss biggg!*" John said, spreading his arms wider and wider. Everyone laughed.

Eric showed them their proposed route on the map. "It's only about five kilometers as the crow flies, but paddling that winding river is likely a good 10 to 15 kilometers. That's enough for the first day, since we're going upstream against the current. However, we only gain about five metres elevation in that distance, so there's very little current to slow us down, as long as there's no wind."

***

They set off at 8 a.m., Julia and John paddling at each end of the canoe, with their dad relaxing and reading in the centre with Buddy. They paddled about two kilometers downriver to where the Coldwater River and Nicola River met, then headed upstream on the Nicola. By 11:30 they were under the Coquihalla Highway, where they stopped for a brief rest. As they bumped ashore, Eric looked up from his book.

"John-boy," said Julia, "you're a good paddler now."

"By gosh, you both are!" said Eric.

Eric gave out snacks from his knapsack, then suggested they paddle on for a while.

Julia and John paddling at each end of the canoe.

Four or five kilometers and half an hour later, Julia said "John, let me know whenever you stop paddling like that. When you halt, I have to compensate, or else we turn at the wrong time."

"I was looking at the water, wondering why there was oil on it," he replied.

"Oil? Where?"

"Right alongside here!"

"Oh, yeah, you're right. Dad, where is this oil coming from? Doesn't that pollute the water?"

Eric looked up from the book he was reading. "What oil are you're talking about?"

"Right here, Dad. See?"

"Hmm, you're right. I wonder where it's coming from. ... Okay, let's see if we can track down the source of the oil."

Eric and Julia continued to paddle upstream for only 100 meters, when they noticed the oil seeping into the river from a wetland. "There! Shove a little way into the reeds and let's find our oil source." They could see that the oil scum was thicker and wider here.

"It looks like it's seeping out of that rocky bank over there."

"Yes, I see," answered her dad. "The pipeline runs under the river nearby, so I wonder if it's coming from a break in that. We must report this to the pipeline company. John, that was very observant of you to notice the oil spill."

"Do we tell the police, Dad?" asked John.

"Let's pull into the shore there where I see some dry land and we'll see if the pipeline crosses here. The main Pacific Western oil pipeline from Alberta to Vancouver runs by the east side of Merritt. There should be a marker post wherever it crosses a highway or a river. So let's look around for those first."

It looks like it's seeping out of that rocky bank over there.
Photo: with permission from Billings Gazette.

"What would a marker look like, Dad?" asked John.

"I believe most oil pipeline markers are white posts with a yellow band and lettering on the top. Let's look on top of the bank here. Julia, why don't you walk along there and see if you find a marker."

***

Eric and John climbed up the grassy slope and found the oil pipeline marker right on top of the bank. "It appears the pipeline may have a break right here," said Eric. He yelled to Julia below that they had found a marker. Meanwhile, Julia was checking out a grassy spot where Buddy was sniffing around, and she came across a small wooden box.

Coming down from the slope, Eric remarked, "We should contact Pacific Western as soon as we're back at camp, and alert them to a potential break in their pipeline. What's that you're holding there, Julia? Did you find that here?"

"Yeah, it's a little wooden box with pictures of a horse and a key engraved on it. Buddy was sniffing at the grass just over there," she said. "And there's a little hand-drawn map inside it." She passed both over to her dad to examine.

Julia found a little wooden box with pictures of a horse and a key engraved on it, and a treasure map inside.

"Maybe it's a map for finding a hidden treasure!" said John.

"It *is* rather mysterious," said their dad. "I wonder what the two symbols mean. And there is a location for something labelled treasure on the map all right."

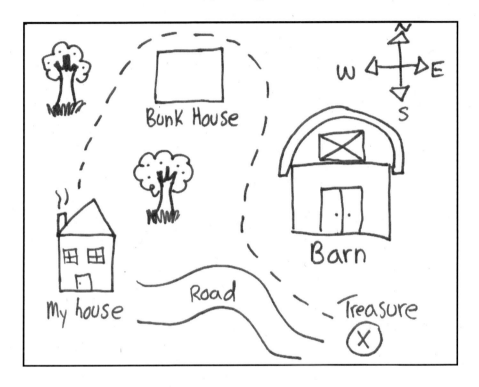

The little box had a treasure map inside.

"Do you think there's any connection to the pipeline break?" asked Julia.

"Not likely. The map looks like it's describing some ranch or other. It represents nothing nearby, so perhaps it just floated here during the spring flood earlier."

"Well, there's no house nearby either, so do you think I can keep it? It's such a pretty little box."

"Sure, that will be okay, Julia," said Eric.

Eric recorded the location using his GPS before getting back in the canoe.

"Let's return to our camp, and perhaps we can solve this mystery."

***

Paddling through the north side of town, they stopped briefly. Eric looked up the number for the Pacific Western Pipeline field office in Kamloops and dialed it. The regional manager in Kamloops answered. "Tom Beasley here."

"Mr. Beasley, my name is Eric Nicholson, from Vancouver. We're vacationing here in Merritt, and this morning my children and I were paddling up the Nicola River. They noticed oil on the water, and we tracked it down to a location where your pipeline crosses under the river. I'm not sure if it's because of a pipeline break, but I'm sure you'd like to check it out."

"I would. Did you get a fix on its location?"

"Yes, I can give you a GPS latitude and longitude, or, if you have someone around Merritt, we can take them to the location."

"The Nicola is a salmon river, so I need to get onto this right away. Could I pick you up this evening?"

"Yes. We're at the Claybanks RV Park, on the south side of town along the Coldwater River. Do you know the spot?"

"Know it well, I've camped there myself. Could I pick you and your kids up about 7 p.m.? You're only an hour away from Kamloops, about 90 kilometres southwest."

"Fine! We're paddling back now and we'll be ready."

***

When they arrived at the campground, John was eager to tell his mom everything they had found out.

"Julia found this little box near an oil spill, with a treasure map inside," he said.

"Really?"

"Dad thinks it's a map of a ranch," Julia interrupted. "There are pictures of a horse and a key inscribed on the cover. Here it is," she replied, as she passed the box over to her mother.

Carol turned the box over. "Interesting," she said, "although I can't imagine what the horse and key mean, and it doesn't have any other information."

"I would just like to know what the treasure is, and the map shows its location," added Julia.

"Let's think on it," said Carol. "Maybe one of you can come up with a theory while we drive out to your oil spill."

***

6. Julia Discovers Oil Leak Source

Tom Beasley arrived sharp at 7 p.m. Eric introduced Tom to Carol, Julia and John. "And this is Buddy", as Buddy sniffed at Tom's shoes.

"So, John and Julia," said Tom. "You're the two young sleuths who discovered this oil, eh?"

"John was the observant one who noticed it first," replied Julia.

"Early discovery and repair of the pipeline could save us trouble. Well, shall we go out to this oil source? Bring Buddy along. I like dogs, and maybe he's good at sniffing out problems."

As they all settled into Beasley's large van, Tom remarked, "I know there's a road along the south side of the Nicola, but the Coquihalla Highway cut off access to it from there. In fact, they renamed the road the Nicola Cutoff Road. We'll drive out Highway 5A to the west end of Nicola Lake, then come back on the cut-off that runs southwest."

Using Eric's GPS location, they found the pipeline markers where it crossed the Cutoff Road, which was only a trail at that point, and parked there. Julia, John and Buddy raced ahead of the adults on the last few hundred metres through a cleared path. Carol called out, "Julia, watch John, that he doesn't fall into the river!"

John and Julia found the pipeline marker above the riverbank right away. The adults arrived a few minutes later. John was eager to point out the oil spill to Mr. Beasley.

After a few minutes, Tom said, "Well, it appears to be a pipeline break; perhaps not so surprising, given that they installed this pipeline in the 1950s. Like most things, our pipelines are more reliable today. I'll have to get our heavy equipment people out to get it repaired right away.

John and Julia found the pipeline marker above the riverbank right away.

Meanwhile Julia and John were checking along the bank downriver, when they noticed Buddy sniffing at a large old oil drum. Julia looked inside and noticed there was still oil at the bottom. "Ooh, this looks important! Let's go tell Mr. Beasley".

Julia blurted out, "Dad, Mr. Beasley, come see what we found, it's an old oil drum! Maybe the oil came from that?" They hurried to where the kids were pointing.

"Hmm", pondered Mr. Beasley. "I wonder...."

"What are you thinking?" asked Eric.

They noticed Buddy sniffing at a large old oil drum.

"Well, we've been laying the new pipeline in various sections, running more or less parallel to this one, waiting on government approval to start it up. We've faced stiff opposition from some folks in this area where we have had to cross their land. We've made agreements with most landowners. However, a few people had concerns about leaks, especially among Nicola and Coldwater bands, just as we suspect here, and they worry that it may poison their farm animals, or worse."

"Are their fears justified?" asked Eric.

"If we were laying a gas pipeline, yes. Then a break and explosion is a possibility if anyone did any digging around the pipeline. But the new pipeline will transport mostly heavy crude oil from the Fort McMurray oil sands."

"And I gather the pipelines are well-marked, correct?"

"Yes, especially where a pipeline crosses a roadway or river, like this location here. Another problem is that once the pipeline is installed, we cannot allow heavy equipment such as farm machinery within ten feet of it. We also keep that safety zone free of trees and shrubs that might cause a break. We compensate farmers for any loss of crops or trees. But some just want no part of it and sometimes cause us genuine problems."

"So, are you thinking this oil leak may be a deliberate attempt to simulate a break?"

"It's possible. They know that leaks like this cause delays. Anyway, I brought along a shovel. Do you mind if I run back to the van to get it and dig a little around this spill? It won't take much time."

"Certainly! We're just as curious about this ourselves."

Five minutes later, Beasley was removing some dirt and gravel around the oil spill. Within minutes, he stood smiling and declared, "This is a plant, to get us concerned enough to get our heavy equipment out here and dig. I think we can call off the heavy equipment, thanks to our young sleuths here again." Turning to Julia and John, he added, "Thank you kids! You've saved us much time and money, and I'll see that you're rewarded for this."

"I think you've rewarded them just by thanking them. They like to help adults anytime they can."

"I believe it. Well, we may as well head back to town. I'll drop you folks off, then report this to the RCMP detachment there. Perhaps they can discover who the mischief-maker might be."

On the way back to Merritt, Eric asked Tom if this was a serious offense.

"Well, no. If I were in their shoes, without much knowledge of the pipeline, it might tempt me to do the same. When a land-owner refuses to give permission for a pipeline across his or her land, we can resort to a process called eminent domain. This means an expropriation of that piece of land as allowed by federal and provincial laws. We then get an independent evaluator to estimate a purchase or rental amount to give the farmer, and he has no choice but to accept it."

"I see," said Eric. "Once they have approved the pipeline, it must go through, regardless of how inconvenient it might be to others."

"That's it. Here we are at your campground. I appreciate the cooperation from all of you on this. How long will you be staying here, Eric?"

"We plan to stay two weeks, if everything goes well."

"The reason I ask is that the RCMP may wish to interview you and the kids. Is that okay?"

"Certainly! Here's my card. You can give them my cell number, since we plan to do some canoeing and fishing over the next few days."

"Ah, *Dr.* Nicholson I see, and you're involved in climate research?"

"That's right."

"Sounds like something I should look into, given my job in the oil industry. Oh, by the way, the kids might like to see the fireworks display tonight at sunset, given that it's the First of July. They have it every year at the rodeo grounds; not much more than a kilometre from here down Lindley Creek Road. Should start in just over an hour."

"Yes, let's go to that," said Julia.

"Sounds like an excellent way to end a busy day. All right, let's grab some camp stools and head down the road."

***

They found a suitable viewing spot at the rodeo grounds. Julia noticed a girl her age right alongside, who smiled at her, so Julia introduced herself.

"Hi, my name's Julia Nicholson. We're visiting here for holidays. Do you live nearby?"

"Yeah, just down the road from here. I'm Leah Holmes, a member of the Coldwater Band here."

Just before the fireworks started, Julia introduced Leah to her family, and mentioned that they would like to get together this week and canoe on the Nicola again.

"Very pleased to meet you, Leah. I'm Carol, this is Julia's dad, Eric, and her brother John".

Just then the first rocket was launched and exploded, so it limited their conversation. Julia and Leah exchanged phone numbers and agreed to meet later in the week to canoe together.

***

7. Mystery Dog

The following morning, Constable Wayne McTavish of the Merritt RCMP contacted Eric. McTavish asked him if he would mind meeting to confirm information on the oil spill. Eric replied that they were just headed into town to pick up some groceries, and they could drop by the RCMP offices after that. They left Buddy in the trailer with windows open and their small air-conditioning unit on and asked the camp owner to monitor their trailer.

A short time later, while leaving the supermarket, Julia and John noticed a small dog in the parking lot. The dog approached the children and licked their hands. Julia checked the dog's collar and found a tag showing its name as *Denny*. Eric suggested that they take the dog to the nearby RCMP detachment, since they were going there to give statements anyway. They drove to the detachment along Voght Street and went inside with the dog in tow on Buddy's spare leash.

Eric spoke to a constable at the desk. "We're here to see Constable McTavish about the oil leak we discovered near the pipeline yesterday. And meanwhile," pointing to the kids who had Denny on a walking leash, "do you have any information on this lost little dog?"

"Yes, I'm Constable McTavish. I spoke to you this morning. And I see you found Denny."
    "You're familiar with him, then?"

Julia and John noticed a small dog in the parking lot.

"Oh, yes," said the officer, "I see Denny's gotten loose again. Gramma Jane Osgoode looks after him. She used to run Gramma Jane's Dog Rescue organization; she's retired now but still takes in stray dogs that we find. We provide her with dog food and our local vet provides any medical care as needed at no cost, and Gramma Jane tries to find the right owners. A camper found Denny at Nicola Lake campground and dropped him off to us about two months ago. Denny keeps escaping from Gramma Jane. We think he's looking for his original owner, a boy or girl like your kids. We can take him back to Gramma Jane's, unless you'd prefer to drop him off yourself afterward; that would be okay too."

"I think the kids themselves would like to see him back at his actual home, so if you can give us Gramma Jane's address, we'll do that."

"In fact, we have copies of her business card with her address right here," and he passed a copy to Eric.

"Now,' the officer continued, "about the oil spill incident; why don't you come inside here to the boardroom? It won't take long; I just need to ask about any other information you may have on the oil spill. Tom Beasley from Pacific Western, whom you met yesterday, will join us."

Just then, Mr. Beasley came in the front door. After greeting one another, Constable McTavish seated them in the boardroom. McTavish started out with, "I understand from Mr. Beasley that Julia and John are budding detectives and discovered the oil spill. And Julia found an oil drum, the source of the spill, not the pipeline?"

"That's correct," said Eric.

"Did either of you notice anything else at the scene, anything that might allow us to trace it back to the culprit?"

"Julia also found a small, wooden box nearby with an odd pair of graphics carved into the cover," Eric explained. It contained a hand-drawn map of a ranch, with an 'X' labeled as treasure. I would say someone about John's age, 8 or 9 drew it.

"Hmm. Doesn't sound like something the chap who spilled the oil would have left around, the officer said. Do you have the box with you, Julia?"

"It's in our car. Would you like to see it?"

"Yes, I would."

Eric passed the car keys to Julia, and she was back a few minutes later with the box.

As she handed the box to the RCMP officer, Julia said, "The cover is engraved with pictures of a horse and a key. The map inside shows a ranch. I wondered whether the pictures suggest the name of the ranch, like Horse-Key, or something similar."

"By gosh, that's it, I'll bet. There is a Horsekey Ranch all right!", said Tom, "it's owned by Walter George of the Coldwater band."

"You mean, I guessed the name right?" Julia said, with all smiles.

"I think so", said Wayne.

Just then, Denny started scratching at the door, and barked once.

"Dad, is it okay if John and I take Denny outside? He looks like he wants to go."

"Watch he doesn't get loose again, Julia," Carol said.

As Julia and John closed the door, Constable McTavish went on, "Walter also has an adolescent daughter, Jenny, about 10, who often accompanies him on his rounds in the area."

"If we're right, it may mean that Walter and his daughter were close to the oil spill location when Jenny lost the little box," added Tom, "unless she lost it on the river and it got washed up on the river bank."

"Tom, do you have any reason to suspect that Walter George is responsible for the oil spill?"

"Possibly . . . Mr. George is not happy with Pacific Western, with good reason I think. My forerunner in this position was over-zealous about the pipeline crossing the Horsekey Ranch; some might call him too pushy. Walter had concerns about the possibility of a pipeline break somehow poisoning his horses. He raises horses for hunting and guiding as you likely know. Anyway, my company pushed the pipeline through his ranch using this eminent domain clause that I explained to Eric yesterday, which upset Mr. George."

"If you turn out to be correct, will you be pressing charges against Walter," asked Constable McTavish?

"Not if I can avoid it. I would not have handled the pipeline right-of-way in that way at all. I'd like to remove any antagonism that's come from this. Just between us, I would not be surprised if Mr. George did plant this oil spill, not just to get even, but to slow things down. If that's the case, even though the act was wrong, I would like to see a better deal for him, and not press charges."

"We could be onto something here. I wonder .... okay, so you think we could resolve this without pressing charges, right?" asked Tom.

"That would be my choice," he continued. "I think we can reassure Mr. George there is no danger to his horses and get him a better financial deal. However, I'm a little reluctant just to approach him myself on his own land. I'm sure he won't wish to speak to me right away, being the current representative of Pacific Western. So how best could we handle this, without the RCMP getting involved?"

"Wait a minute. Perhaps I can suggest something," Eric said. "I'm sure Julia would like to return the little box to Jenny, his daughter. What if we met Walter and returned the box? We could mention that we found it near an oil leak on the Nicola River, that I told Pacific Western about a leak, and that we took Mr. Beasley to the site. He will mention his disagreement with Pacific Western, perhaps point out his own part in this. If so, I could then mention that Tom, the new field officer from Pacific Western, feels that Walter got a raw deal on the pipeline crossing, and that he would like to renegotiate it."

"Excellent," Tom said. "However, are you certain you want to get involved?"

"I don't see why not," Eric replied. "We're already involved anyway, and this is a subject that interests Carol. Right, dear?"

"Yes, I'm in the middle of writing a book on pipelines and how they might affect First Nations bands in B.C. I want to get viewpoints from both First Nations and Pacific Western. What better way than to get involved in this and get excellent information from both sides."

"Great, this could be a win-win all around", exclaimed Constable McTavish. "Eric, I'll get you a phone number so you can call ahead. Mention that Julia guessed the ranch name, and the RCMP provided you with his contact information - no deception there. You're under no obligation, so you don't have to feel you are being our investigator. There's no harm or dishonesty involved in your telling him what you know, and that you've spoken with Tom here yourself.

"This just might work out okay," Tom added with a smile.

"Tom," the officer said, "you'll be contacting Mr. George at some point anyway to see if he's interested in the renegotiation. But wait until the Nicholsons meet them. Does this fit into your plans?"

"Absolutely!"

"Well, let's see what happens in the next few days. I hope we can get together on this again," said Constable McTavish.

After the officer found Walter George's phone number for Eric, they all shook hands again, and as Eric and his family and Tom headed toward the door, McTavish added, "Eric and Carol, did you know the town has a fairground event this Saturday at the Rodeo grounds? It features many entertainment venues for children. You might enjoy it."

"Yes," replied Eric. "Carol mentioned that to me this morning, and we plan to attend."

A few minutes later, they knocked on Gramma Jane's door.

A smiling lady in her 70s answered and noticed Denny. "Ah, you found my wandering little angel. I suppose the RCMP gave you my address?"

"Yes", replied Julia.

"Then thank you so much for returning him. I wish we could find the owner. I wouldn't mind keeping this darling little fellow, but I feel certain that some little boy or girl is broken-hearted from losing him, and I hope we can track them down soon."

"Yes, Constable McTavish told us how you came to have Denny," Julia said.

"The RCMP bring all strays to me, but they also supply me with lots of nutritious dog food," said Gramma Jane. She continued, "I've put notices on Denny up all over town and advertised in the local paper, but I guess the owners have never seen those."

Gramma Jane served them tea and cookies, and they had chatted for about an hour when Carol remembered their groceries left in the heated car. They excused themselves, said goodbye, and headed back to the campground.

Given all their talk and activities around oil spills, Carol and Eric took the kids to see the movie, *Dead Ahead: The Exxon Valdez Disaster*, a special showing at the local library. It was a dramatization of the massive 1989 oil spill in Prince William Sound, Alaska. The entire family enjoyed it, and it clarified several questions that John and Julia had.

***

8. The HorseKey Ranch

The next morning, Eric called Walter George.

"Hullo, Walter George here, Horsekey Ranch."

"Hi Mr. George. My name is Eric Nicholson. My family and I are spending a two-week vacation around Merritt. Yesterday, we were canoeing on the Nicola River east of Merritt, and my daughter, Julia, found a box that has a horse and a key inscribed on the cover. Because of a hand-drawn map of a ranch inside the box, she suggested a ranch called *Horsekey*. We checked with the RCMP in town and found this link to your ranch. We assumed that it belongs to one of your children, and Julia would love to stop by and return it if it's yours."

"Oh, you bet!" said Walter, clearly relieved. He continued, "There's a story behind that little box, and I know my daughter - Jenny is her name - would love to have it back. Her grandpa made that for Jenny, and she is fond of it. Could you drop by sometime for lunch? We'd like to meet you and your family, and we'll tell you the story."

"That would be nice. We could come out tomorrow, or even today, whatever is convenient for you."

"Today would be perfect!" Walter said, adding, "we're about 15 kilometres northeast of Merritt, as the crow flies that is. You need to take Highway 5A straight off Voght Street, not the Coquihalla; then drive about eight kilometres east from the overpass. A little past the Nicola Ranch (you can't miss that one), you'll find the Mill Creek Road that runs north. Take the Mill Creek until you reach a fork at about kilometre 2.5; stay on the left branch. You have to slow down then for two sharp 180-degree turns, left, then right; then continue until you run right into our ranch. You'll see the overhead sign, Horsekey Ranch. Call me at this same number if you get lost."

"Sounds simple enough. We can see you around about noon. Is that okay? And do you mind if we bring our dog? We don't like to leave him locked up too long."

"Hey," Walter replied, "a ranch is for animals, so bring your dog. It should be excellent therapy for Jenny, as she lost hers some time back. We'll look forward to meeting you and your family, Mr. Nicholson."

They had no trouble finding the Horsekey Ranch. As they drove onto the property, Walter and his family came outside to greet them.

Home of the Georges at Horsekey Ranch.

"Hello Eric," said Walter, "and this must be Julia, you mentioned her name. This is my wife Annie, our daughter Jenny, and son Will."

"Hi," smiled Eric, "and this is my wife Carol, daughter Julia, son John, and Buddy," nodding towards the dog.

Walter said, "Well, Jenny here can't contain herself since you mentioned Julia finding her little treasure box. Come on inside. We have the coffee pot on and some lemonade for the kids."

"So tell me your background, Eric," said Walter.

"Yes, I'm on faculty at the University of Vancouver. I study climate change. Carol is a meteorologist, a weather forecaster with Environment Canada. We've been promising the kids a holiday, camping, fishing, and canoeing for some time now. We came to the Merritt area for holidays. All of us enjoy canoeing, and both the Coldwater and Nicola Rivers have gentle canoeing runs. Also, I've heard that both rivers have salmon and trout."

"Oh, do they ever! You came to the right place for all of those."

"Carol is also a writer," explained Eric, "and wanted to spend a little quiet time doing some research for her book while the kids amuse their dad."

At that moment, Annie brought in coffee and lemonade on a tray. "We'll have lunch in a short while - would you like smoked salmon?"

"That would be excellent," replied Carol. "We like salmon, especially smoked."

"What are you writing about, Carol?" asked Walter.

"I'm doing some background writing on the Pacific Western pipeline, how it came about, and how it affects First Nations, all those considerations."

"Annie and I have some personal involvement there that you may want to hear about."

"Wonderful," replied Carol.

While the adults had coffee, the four children drank lemonade and talked among themselves. Julia brought out the little box belonging to Jenny and passed it over to her.

"Here you go, Jenny. All it contained was your little map. Was there anything else in the box when you lost it?"

"No, that's all."

"I notice you wrote treasure on a spot on your map."

"Yes, it is buried treasure, for me anyway. Would you like to see my treasure place?"

"Sure", said Julia and John together.

"Well, c'mon, I'll show you."

***

9. Confession

The adults had been listening to the children's conversation up to this point. As the children went outside, Annie said, "Jenny had a little dog, a little terrier. She was close to her dog, and it followed her everywhere, except to school. About two months ago, he disappeared while she was in school. We searched and called everywhere for him, checked on the sides of the roads, even the Coquihalla. We suspect someone picked him up and claimed him. It devastated Jenny to lose him, and she blames herself, although we've convinced her it's no one's fault. Anyway, her grandmother had given her a little gold locket, and Jenny kept a picture of her dog in the locket, so he was always with her. A week after she lost him, Jenny took the locket and buried it over on a corner of the ranch, then drew a map of its location and put it in that little box. Her grandfather made that little box for her and engraved the horse and key on it. So she was carrying the box around with her, but a week ago she came home and said she no longer had the box and couldn't recall where she might have left it."

"Where *did* Julia find the box?" asked Annie.

"Well, that's a story too," said Eric. "Two days ago we were canoeing on the Nicola, when John noticed an oil slick on the water. Earlier in the month, we had been talking about different water pollution sources, and so he noticed the oil right away. We tracked the oil slick down to its source. It appeared to result from a break where the pipeline crosses under the river. While poking around the site, Julia found the box. I thought it might have floated downstream during spring flooding, since it's a remote spot for a little girl to have been. Then Julia discovered this empty oil container. Someone may have dumped oil on the riverbank."

"Ohh, ... now I know how this came about," said Walter. "Well, how do I explain this?" He paused a few moments while collecting his thoughts.

"We've had this on-going battle with Pacific Western Pipelines because their pipeline runs right through our land. My concern was that I heard that pipeline breaks sometimes release poisonous gases that could kill my horses. I recall hearing about a rancher in the Alberta foothills a few years ago who was away for a weekend with his family. There was a blowout from a gas pipeline on his pastures, and they found 200 dead cattle when they arrived home. It was hydrogen sulfide gas released in the explosion that killed the cattle, but the gas company refused to admit fault. Pacific Western offered us compensation to grant them permission, but their explanation and lack of safety guarantees didn't satisfy us, so we turned them down. However, they went ahead with the pipeline despite our objections, claiming an eminent domain clause that allowed them to build with or without our permission. I checked with a lawyer, and it is legal, but I'm still not happy about it. Meanwhile, I can't use my land within ten meters either side of the pipeline. I can't drive over the pipeline, and they refused to build a bridge across it. They violated our rights. I appealed to both the federal and provincial governments, I wrote to my MP, my MLA, and to newspapers, the whole gamut, but nothing has worked so far."

"I must confess that, in an act of frustration, I was the one who dumped that oil there, and I was waiting for someone to find it. If they suspected an oil pipeline break, perhaps I would get more attention to my case. Jenny was with me that day and must have left her little box down there. I guess the good Lord has strange ways of making your sins find you out!"

"Most likely we'll wind up in court over this on some pollution charge or other," added Annie, "but I support my husband. We hope to get some positive media attention, and maybe then something can be achieved."

"So what assurances did Pacific Western give you there was no danger?" asked Carol.

"Nothing at all. The regional manager said there is no danger, and left it at that, no further explanation. The technicians they sent in to install the pipeline were friendly and polite enough, but they were just doing the job they were paid to do and couldn't provide any clarification. But Eric, for us this is a very *inconvenient pipeline.*"

"I have to tell you, Walter," Eric began, "that we reported the oil spill to Pacific Western in Kamloops. The new regional manager there, Tom Beasley, drove down and went out with us to view the spill. That's when Julia discovered the empty oil drum. Mr. Beasley then dug around the spot and determined the oil spill did not come from the pipeline. I should mention that Mr. Beasley is sympathetic towards you on this. He took over as the new regional field manager. The company felt the previous chap, the one you dealt with, was too aggressive with people. I believe Beasley would like to renegotiate the entire business with you. He's not interested in pressing charges against you. In fact, he said he might have done the same if it was his property. I should add that he did not put us up to contacting you. That was my idea after Julia guessed that the little box came from your ranch. But he mentioned that he would try to contact you himself."

"Well, that would be a welcome change of pace," said Annie. "Walter, we must hear what this Mr. Beasley has to say."

"Yes, for sure. There's no harm in hearing him out. . . . You know, Eric, I would be more comfortable if you could sit in with us on that discussion."

"If Mr. Beasley is agreeable, I'd be more than willing to meet with you both. We're here for two weeks and have lots of free time. I'd be delighted to help any way I can."

***

10. Mystery Treasure Restored

Meanwhile, the children and Buddy had reached the buried treasure site. Jenny had a small garden spade, and after digging away a few inches of dry soil, she removed a board and brought up a covered tin can. She opened the lid and removed a gold chain and a heart-shaped locket. "This is my treasure," she said proudly.

She opened the locket, and inside was a picture of a small dog. "But this was my real treasure," Jenny said, "except he ran away. I miss him terribly," and she sobbed a little.

Julia's heart almost stopped, for she thought she recognized the little dog. "What was your dog's name?" she asked.

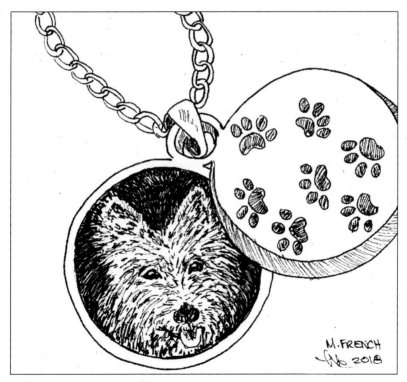

"What was your dog's name?" she asked.

"Denny," said Jenny, "and I loved him so much."

Julia put her hand to her mouth, then exclaimed, "Omigosh, Jenny, we know where Denny is! A wonderful old lady in Merritt known as Gramma Jane is looking after him for you. She used to run a dog rescue home and still looks after strays the RCMP pick up. Some camper on Nicola Lake, where Denny must have wandered, dropped him off at the RCMP office, and they passed him on to Gramma Jane. She was so sure that someone like you would look for Denny and left notices all over town, but I guess no one recognized Denny."

"Are you sure? Are you certain that it's Denny?" Jenny demanded.

"It must be, because he looks just like this, and the name tag on his collar says Denny. We found him on the street and brought him to the RCMP, and they directed us to Gramma Jane who looks after lost dogs."

"Oh, thank you, thank you!" and Jenny jumped into Julia's arms and hugged her fiercely. "I have to go tell Mom and Dad right away," and off she raced with the other three trailing behind her.

"Mom, Dad! Mom, Dad! Julia has found Denny! We have to leave right away and get him!"

"Slow down, child. What are you saying?" said Annie, as Julia, John, and Will came into the room. "How did Julia find her?" She looked towards Julia expectantly. Julia quickly explained once again how they found Denny.

"Jenny is right. We need go to right away, or this child will never settle down. Did you get a phone number for this lady, Mr. Nicholson?"

"Yes, it's on her business card," he said as he passed it to Annie.

"Here, Walter, call this number right now."

Five minutes later, they were all in two vehicles headed back to Merritt, forgetting all about the lunch that Annie had prepared.

***

They were all ushered into Gramma Jane's house. Seeing the joy on Jenny's face and in Denny's reaction to Jenny, Gramma Jane remarked, "It's obvious that there's no question about whose dog this is; you don't even need to show any identification. Those two," pointing to Jenny holding on to Denny, "have provided that better than any paperwork. I'm overjoyed to see them together; this just made my day, makes my job worthwhile!"

"Well," said Walter George, "Annie and I are also pleased about this happy ending. And we insist that you allow us to take you all to lunch, since that was how we started out about an hour ago."

"That would be lovely," answered Gramma Jane.

"We'll take you to the new Coldwater Restaurant, run by our band," said Annie. "They have a Chinook salmon dish that's to die for, served with bannock or corn bread."

"That sounds like a real treat," said Carol.

"You've made me hungry already," added Eric.

***

11. A Better Deal for Ranchers

Later, as they relaxed with tea and coffee in a private meeting room in the restaurant, they traded stories about their lives in a roundtable setting. While they were talking, Walter received a call from Tom Beasley on his cell phone. He was smiling when he turned off his phone.

"That sounded pleasant enough," remarked Eric.

"Yes, I'm happy with his offer. He's still in Merritt, and he will drop over here right away to discuss it. You will stay, Eric?"

"Yes" he replied.

Annie suggested that she and Carol and Gramma Jane take the kids to the nearby public library where there was a special program on for children, including a puppet show. Carol agreed.

"The men can meet us afterward," Annie said.

Walter reviewed the offer that Tom had made over the phone. "What do you think, Eric?"

"Sounds good to me, but you best know your own operation. Will they guarantee protection for your horses, as remote as a serious break may be?"

Walter nodded. "He explained that if a break in the oil pipeline should occur, it would trigger a warning to their field base. We would be compensated for any loss of horses should the worst situation occur, but that's unlikely. They've doubled the land rental, and will also pay for any fencing, and a wooden bridge over the pipeline, strong enough to handle trucks and horses.

Tom joined Eric and Walter afterward, and they ordered up more coffee.

"So," Tom began, "did you discuss my offer with Eric?"

"Yes, and we both think it's fair. The only question I have is how likely is a pipeline break?"

"We've had only ten pipeline breaks over several thousand kilometers of pipeline in the past ten years. Almost all were because of negligence, usually heavy equipment operators digging without calling us first. Only one incident involved a gas line break where several head of cattle were poisoned. But the pipeline through your property is for oil anyway."

"That sounds like good odds in my favour, wouldn't you agree, Eric?"

"I agree, and you seem happy with the monetary side, right?"

"Yes, because we'll be able to cross the pipeline and get to our northwest quarter where there's plenty of grazing meadow. I'd say we have a deal, Tom," and he offered his hand.

After handshakes all around, Tom added, "Now, Eric, I have something to tell you about your little detectives. I've discussed this with our head office and suggested that your kids deserve a reward."

"I was serious when I told you that both kids felt rewarded just by being told that they were helpful. But, if you think it's good publicity for your company, then I'm sure that Carol and I won't mind."

"The company agreed on two scholarship funds placed into a registered education savings plan for them, $10,000 for Julia, who will need it soonest, and $5,000 for John. You can add to those whenever you wish."

Eric smiled broadly with "Now that reward we don't mind. These kids are bright, and they'll likely go to university. Julia has finished Grade 8, and John only Grade 4. They're both some years away from university. A registered education savings plan can gain much interest in four and eight years, which is the time they have ahead to complete high school."

"I mentioned this so you won't be surprised at the rodeo grounds this weekend. The city also plans to recognize them, and the mayor and Constable McTavish will do that. They'll also recognize the kids for finding Jenny's dog and recognizing the ranch."

"I don't think they will get too swelled in the head over all this, but thank you for doing this and letting me know in advance."

"The reward is for finding the oil leak and saving our company time and money by not having to repair the pipeline. Walter, your minor misdemeanour won't even be mentioned. You helped raise more awareness, and that resulted in our agreement tonight. It also gives our company a better means of dealing with First Nations bands over pipelines. So you did us a favour, and I mean that."

"Well, the band will also be happy that we've set a precedent with this agreement, which bodes well for First Nations people all along the pipeline route from Alberta to Burnaby."

"It's a win-win", Eric added.

"Sure is," agreed Tom.

***

12. The Young Mystery Drifter

The following morning, Carol worked on her book project again for a while, having picked up plenty of material over the past week, mostly from Annie. John was playing with a boy his age in the camp playground, so Eric and Julia took Buddy for a walk downriver toward the confluence with the Nicola. "It's about one and a half kilometers as the crow flies," said Eric, "but closer to two kilometres if the crow has to walk it," He added. Their golden retriever, Buddy, loved to chase sticks and run pell-mell with it back and forth, then disappear for a few seconds at a time.

After one such run, Julia was surprised to see Buddy down on the riverbank alongside somebody sitting there. The person was motionless, and Buddy walked up to him and started licking his face.

"Uh, oh. Buddy, come!" she yelled. Eric pulled out a whistle and blew two shorts and a long, which, as always, caused Buddy to whip around and dash back to them. Julia slipped Buddy's leather choke collar over his head. The person still had not moved. "We should check on that person, Dad. Maybe he's injured, or even dead."

"You're right, Julia. You stay here a few moments, while I check on him." Eric spoke up while approaching, and asked, "Are you okay there?"

A young man in his late teens turned to Eric, pointing a revolver in his direction, and said, "No, I'm not okay at all, so leave me alone."

The person appeared motionless, and Buddy walked up to him and was licking his face (Photo: G. Strong).

"Whoa, please don't point that revolver towards me! I'm just concerned for your welfare. Our dog just walked up and licked your face. I apologize for that, but golden retrievers show instinctive care for humans."

"Why should you care for me? No one else does! But I love dogs, so I didn't mind that at all. Your dog gave me more attention than any human has in a long while."

"Look, do you mind if I sit and talk with you a while? I'm a good listener."

"Suit yourself, not that it changes anything."

"Well, let's start with introductions. My name is Eric, Eric Nicholson. That's my daughter, Julia, up there with Buddy," pointing to Julia.

"Yeah, well, why don't you call her down here too?" the young man asked.

"Only if you put that gun away."

"Oh, that, well, I may as well toss it," he said, as he threw the revolver into the river. "I've never handled a gun in my life. You know, I had planned to end my life right here, but I got thinking, what if some small kid discovered my body later with my brains shot out? It wouldn't be proper for a young kid to see that, would it?"

"No, but that shows you still have judgment and concern for others, nothing wrong about that." Eric waved at Julia and motioned her to come down. Seconds later, he introduced her. "So this is Julia, and I'm sorry, but I didn't catch your name."

"I'm Jason, Jason Wells," and he shook hands with both Eric and Julia, then ruffled Buddy's head. "Gosh, you sure have a beautiful dog here!"

"Sometimes that's all that saves him," said Julia. "His good looks I mean, because he is so hard to train! He just feels the need to run up to everyone to tell them he loves them in his own way, and he still does not listen to our commands until after he greets strangers. Not everyone likes dogs. Still, we wouldn't trade him for anything in the world. Right, Dad?"

"Yes, that's true. . . . Jason, do you live here?"

"No. I left Red Deer, Alberta last summer, just to get away, wound up in Kamloops. Took a few jobs, made some new friends, but they were too much into drugs. . . . I guess I didn't look after myself, and I didn't make much money at part-time jobs, not enough to rent a place, anyway. I didn't want to stay with those friends or I'd be doing the same drugs. I hid out under a bridge and made do as best I could until the winter set in. Then living like that got rough. I could stay at the Salvation Army community services place on the coldest nights. Everywhere else I tried, nobody wanted me around, because I guess I was dishevelled - like I am now. So last May I hitched a ride down here to Merritt, but it's turned out little better, and I'm, well, feeling very depressed."

"Do your parents know where you are," offered Julia?

"That's another unpleasant part of my story. My parent's marriage broke up in Calgary where we lived about six years ago, when I was 13, or I should say, my mother broke it up. Dad was too busy, I guess. Mom took me to Red Deer but never spent much time home. After a few years, she took off with this guy, and I haven't seen her since. Guess I'm not too important to her."

"How about your dad? Have you contacted him?"

"No. He used to visit me often in Red Deer, but Mom wouldn't let me visit him in Calgary, so we never had much time together. I didn't want to contact him after Mom left, so I stayed with friends, got into trouble with drugs and alcohol . . . Say, Julia, can I offer you some advice? Never, never try that stuff."

"I have no intention of ever trying drugs, and alcohol doesn't interest me either. I've seen kids my age come to school after a weekend binge, wasted. It looks so disgusting, and those people never do well in school either."

"I'm not sure how, with all the trouble we had, but I completed my high school before I came out to B.C."

"That's a good start right there, Jason. We can help you get in contact with your dad, if you wish."

"Well, maybe later, not right away. I feel so ashamed of myself, and I'd rather get myself a job first, if someone would take me, but everywhere I tried here, no one wanted to even talk to me. Guess I don't look too reliable as I am."

"Have you tried the Salvation Army here in Merritt? They

could help you with clothes and meals and find you a place to stay."

"I tried, but I guess I talked to the wrong person. He turned me away."

"Tell you what. Come on with us right now. We'll take you to Tim Horton's or McDonald's for lunch, whichever you prefer. You look like you could use a meal for starters. Then we'll help you find a place to stay. How does that sound?"

"Best offer I've heard all day, in fact the only offer I've had in a few months. I like McDonald's. But, sorry, I don't have any money myself."

"You don't worry about that," said Julia. "C'mon Jason, let's go," and she offered him her hand to get up.

Eric called Carol and told her they were taking a young man to lunch, and he would explain later. After eating lunch and checking several locations, they found Jason a place to stay for a few nights in a Salvation Army hostel. Eric promised him they would drop back the next morning and help him find some better clothes and a local job.

***

Later that afternoon, the Nicholsons drove west past the rodeo grounds to a trout pool that Walter had recommended to Eric. Eric and Julia explained how they had met Jason, took him to lunch, and found him a temporary place to stay. "He seems like a good kid. He's had a rough time and needs a decent break."

Julia added, "He likes Buddy, and Buddy likes him, so he must be okay."

Carol asked Eric, "Are you going to see him tomorrow and help him find a job?"

"I'll at least ask around for him."

After locating the trout pool, Eric decided to just sit and read a while. Carol went through a few pointers with Julia and John on attaching flies. Then they each picked a spot along the riverbank.

Carol was first to make a catch, a beautiful rainbow trout, followed by Julia who also caught one. John, feeling a little frustrated, was bemoaning his lack of nibbles when his rod dipped and he let out a yell!

Carol was first to make a catch, a beautiful rainbow trout.

"Keep your cool, John," called Carol. "Let him play out a few feet, then lift your rod, that's it, you have him on. Now reel in."

John followed his mom's advice and brought the large trout in close to shore where Carol could help him land it. Within an hour, they had a half dozen good-sized trout, enough to make a good meal for them. Carol thought it was time to head back.

"Looks like John caught the largest trout", remarked Julia. John beamed with pride.

After exploring a little further downstream, they drove back to camp. Eric cleaned the fish with John looking on, while Carol and Julia prepared other dishes for dinner. All their discussions focused on the young man, Jason.

During dinner, Carol remarked to Eric, "I hope you won't mind that Annie is coming by at seven, and we're stepping out for coffee to discuss our writing projects. We'll be back before nine. We thought you and Walter might like to get together while us girls step out."

"Why, that's great, dear! Part of your project involves First Nations, and given that both Walter and Annie sit on the Nicola Tribal Association gives you access to much more information. Meanwhile, I'll discuss Jason's problem of finding a job. Perhaps there are ranchers nearby who need help for the summer."

"Yes, and I might provide Annie some updated information on Pacific Western and pipelines, plus information I have from other bands in southern B.C."

"Walter and I agree that it would be great if you two wrote something together, even a magazine article."

Carol smiled. "Hmm, who knows!"

***

Later, Eric explained Jason's problem to Walter and asked him about possibilities in the Nicola Valley.

"Look no further, my friend. I need help with fencing, now that we have a deal with Pacific Western. I can give him a job, and he can stay in the bunkhouse we have next to the barn. Can only pay him about $15 an hour, but he'd have free room and board. My new deal with Pacific Western will pay part of his salary."

"By gosh, that would be perfect! We'll pick him up tomorrow morning before heading to the rodeo grounds, find him some clothes and stuff. Then we can drop him off with you, assuming he is interested, which I'm certain he will be."

"Why don't you bring him along to the rodeo grounds? I can talk with him there, and everyone can enjoy the day."

"Perfect. Another coffee?"

"You're on," said Walter.

***

13. Awards and Rewards

On Saturday morning, Eric and Julia picked up Jason and got him some clothes from the Salvation Army Thrift Store. Then he explained the job offer to Jason.

"My gosh, that sounds better than anything I'd hoped for. I'll take it for sure! You know, you folks have been good to me. I'm grateful, and I promise someday I'll make it up to you."

Julia cut in with, "I think we have Buddy to thank for this. Without him greeting you with big dog kisses, maybe this would not have happened."

"Yes, maybe without Buddy, I would not even be here."

"Let's not think about that anymore," said Eric. "We have lots to be thankful for. Jason, never feel embarrassed about any of your problems. In a situation like you had, I say, *there but for the grace of God go I.* It could happen to anyone if you don't have support around you."

By 9:30 a.m., they had all packed into the Toyota and were heading to the rodeo just two kilometres from their campground. There they met the George family, and Eric introduced Walter and Jason. The two went off together to discuss some details while the others started taking in the activities, including a farm animal petting zoo, ring toss games, balloons and darts, basketball, and so on. During the morning, Julia met up with Leah again, and they both took charge of the three younger children. Julia and Leah made plans to canoe the Nicola River for a few hours the following morning, starting out from the campground.

Walter rejoined them at 11:30, and said to Eric, "Well, Jason has a job, and I've got me a ranch hand. And I got a bonus, because Jason did some fencing while in Red Deer, so it won't take long to show him what needs doing. He was keen to start as soon as possible, so I just drove him back to the ranch where he can pile up posts and fencing for Monday."

"Wonderful. On another issue, I've been meaning to say I'm glad that Tom did not single you out as having planted that oil spill," Eric remarked. "I would have been uncomfortable with that, being the one who alerted them. Besides, like Tom said, you did everyone a favour by drawing attention to the raw deals dealt to some ranchers and farmers."

"Perhaps so, although I can't help wondering whether I could have taken a milder approach."

"I don't think complaining would have moved the company to do anything different, unless it involved Mr. Beasley. You were the impetus that got the company to improve its relationship with the locals."

"True, I suppose."

At lunch time, Tom Beasley joined the Nicholsons and Georges to have hot dogs and pop for lunch. Halfway through lunch, the mayor of Merritt came on the microphone with RCMP Constable McTavish. "Good afternoon, ladies and gentlemen and boys and girls. It's time now for our *citizen of the year* award and to pay honour to the winner. I will ask Constable McTavish to explain the procedure. The winner is not a resident of Merritt this year, but this person helped to solve two puzzling mysteries in our town, and it involved the RCMP in both. Constable McTavish?"

"Thank you Mayor, and good afternoon everyone. This year, Merritt Council agreed the citizen of the year award would go to a young person who is not a resident of Merritt, but happens to be visiting this week. So, I would like to call that person, a young lady forward. Julia Nicholson, please step up onto the stage."

"Omigosh, Mom, Dad! He doesn't mean me, does he?"

"I think so, Julia," said Eric. "Go ahead and speak your best."
Julia walked up to the stage.

The mayor was holding a special plaque, and he addressed Julia. "Julia, on behalf of the Merritt Town Council, and all Merritt residents, we recognize you for solving several mysteries, including that of a small oil spill on our Nicola River. Many farmers and ranchers draw water from the river for their crops and livestock, so people ought to alert us to even small spills. Julia, with help from her brother, John, also discovered the owner of a little dog called Denny. John, please stand up so the crowd can see you. Denny had been in and out of Gramma Jane's dog rescue home for the past two months. He was escaping every other day in trying to find his young master. Julia solved this mystery by working out the name of the ranch where Denny belongs, the Horsekey Ranch of Walter and Annie George. Denny's owner is none other than Jenny George! Jenny, would you also stand up? . . . Thank you, John and Jenny, and thank you, Julia for all your sleuthing work. We therefore present this plaque to Julia Nicholoson to acknowledge her as the environmental citizen of the year for the town of Merritt."

The mayor passed the plaque to Julia while shaking her hand. The audience applauded.

Then the mayor asked, "Would you like to say something to the audience?"

Speaking into the microphone, Julia said: "Yes, I'd like to mention that it was my younger brother, John here, who first noticed the oil slick on the river. Our dad had taught us about pollution and knew who to contact. So we both thank you for this award."

Constable McTavish added: "Maybe the RCMP could use you two when you are a few years older." More applause followed.

Julia, on behalf of the Merritt Town Council, and all Merritt residents, we recognize you as 'Citizen of the Year' for solving the mystery of oil pollution on our Nicola River.

The mayor regained the microphone. "Now, for those of you who do not know him, may I also introduce Mr. Tom Beasley, who is just coming on the stage. Tom recently took over as regional field manager for Pacific Western Pipelines in Kamloops. He is responsible for the pipelines that run by Merritt, and he was quick to determine that the remuneration forced on Walter and Annie George was very unfair. I understand that Mr. Beasley has an extra reward for our two sleuths, a valuable award, I understand. Mr. Beasley, the floor is yours."

"Thank you Mayor and Constable McTavish. Well, it's not common that an oil leak near a pipeline turns out to have a source other than the pipeline. John noticed the oil slick on the water, then Julia discovered its source, which was from a deliberate spill. The spill was not enough to cause serious environmental damage, but their sleuthing saved us from bringing in heavy equipment to carry out an expensive repair that was unnecessary. In appreciation for their concern for the environment, the company is awarding $10,000 into an education fund for Julia Nicholson, and $5,000 into a similar fund for John Nicholson. Those registered education savings funds will be worth far more by the time Julia and John attend university. Julia, please accept this paper documenting the rewards and a thank-you letter from Pacific Western."

More applause followed. Julia and John returned to their table, their heads held high and their ears burning.

Tom came down to tell the Nicholsons that he would drop by Sunday morning to bring the formal paperwork for Julia and John's education funds.

The Georges added their congratulations to Julia and John, and Jenny gave Julia an enormous hug. Then she put her perspective forward by stating, "Julia should have gotten another award for finding my little Denny, because that was most important of all, and Julia is my hero!"

"I'll second that," added Annie. "Jenny, perhaps you can reward Julia and John by asking them along with their mom and dad out to the ranch to go horseback riding."

"Oh, would you, Julia?"

"Yes, I would love to go horseback riding, but you must teach me how to ride a horse."

"Why don't we do that Monday," added Walter. "What do you say, Carol and Eric?"

"That's a splendid idea," said Carol, "and I think Eric will agree,".

Eric glanced at Julia and John. "I think it will delight the kids, and it's their holiday, so I'm game."

"Well, it's decided then," Walter declared. "And Leah, if it's okay with your parents, you come along too."

"Wow, that's cool. Thanks."

"Whoo-hoo!" Julia whooped, and Jenny followed suit.

***

14. The Prodigal Son

Leah arrived at 8:30 on Sunday morning. Because Julia planned to take John and Buddy on their short canoe trip, Eric had the canoe roped down on the Toyota to transport over to the Nicola River at the Lions Memorial Park in town, as he was concerned that the two girls alone might find themselves in trouble navigating at the Nicola-Coldwater confluence. He dropped the kids and Buddy off with the canoe, agreeing to pick them up at the same location at noon. Back at the campground, Eric and Carol took a short walk along the river to relax. They talked about the good things that had happened since they had arrived on the previous Monday. Carol said, "Yes, the week has been more than just eventful."

Later that morning about 10:30, Tom Beasley dropped by with the paperwork for the savings funds. He looked a little downcast, so Carol, at a wink from Eric, asked him to stay for coffee. They talked about the pipeline and the previous day's awards. Then Eric asked, "Do you have a family, Tom?"

"Well, yes and no," he replied. "What I mean is, my wife and I broke up some years back, and I guess I still have some regrets."

"Did you have children?" Carol asked.

"Yes, a son, and therein lies most of my regrets."

"How so?" asked Carol.

"Well, we lived in Calgary where I worked for Pacific Western. I was plenty busy all the time, and I'm responsible for our marriage breakdown because of that. But worse, I didn't pay enough attention to my son, and that I regret most of all."

"What happened to him?"

"My wife left with him for Red Deer. He was still only 12 or

13 and I was still travelling a lot for the company, often overseas. Oh, I went to Red Deer often, and took him out a bit, but once kids become teenagers, if you haven't bonded by then, chances are you've lost the game. His mother would not let him join me in Calgary, even when I was home."

Eric felt his skin tingling, and he glanced over at Carol who was feeling the same.

"So, where is your son now?" asked Eric.

"Well, after a few years, my ex-wife met someone else. She went off with this new guy; to where I've no idea. She never told me, nor did she suggest any arrangements she made for our son. I was managing a new pipeline construction in Saudi Arabia for three months early last year. As soon as I got back to Calgary last summer, I went to Red Deer and found both my wife and son had left their apartment, but with no forwarding address. I found some of my son's friends, who told me Jason had gone out to central B.C., in Kamloops or nearby."

"Hmm, well what did you do then?"

"I went back to Calgary, saw my boss, and pleaded with him to transfer me to Kamloops, as that field manager position had just come open. He agreed, and you know the rest of the story to this point. But I still haven't been able to track down my son, and given all the drug problems these days, I'm worried sick about him."

"What's your son's name?"

"Jason."

"Hmm, I know a young man by that name, about 19 or 20 years old, I'd say. In fact, Julia and I just met him on Friday, a very depressed young man, but his last name is Wells, Jason Wells, not Beasley."

"Omigosh!" cried out Tom. "That's him! His mother had

his name changed back to her maiden name of Wells after they went to Red Deer. Good Lord, where is he now?"

"Tom, you won't believe this set of coincidences, but he's now working for Walter George. He just started last evening. I must tell you the whole story later, but we should call him. He'd like to get in touch with you, but he was in such a bad state on Friday that he wanted to first get his life straightened out and find a job before he looked you up, not knowing you were in this area. I think he didn't want to be forced to beg from you—like the prodigal son in the Bible. But I think so much good has come from our meeting him in just three days that it would excite him to meet with you right now. Would you like me to call him first to test the waters?"

"Oh gosh, yes! Please do."

Eric dialed Walter's number.

"Hello", Walter answered.

"Hi Walter, it's Eric here. Is Jason anywhere nearby? Could you get him to call me back as soon as possible?"

"He's right here with us, Eric. We're just sitting down for Sunday brunch. Hang on. I'll get him for you."

"Hello", said Jason.

"Jason, I know you've gone through some shocking—but good—changes in the past three days. I have another shock for you, but it's a pleasant one."

"Oh, and what would that be?"

"Well, I have someone here to speak with you. I'll put him on."

Tom took Eric's cell and spoke. "Hello, son".

"Dad? Is that you?"

"Yes, it is."

"Omigosh! Can you come out here, Dad? I need to talk with you!"

"And I you. Ask Walter if it's okay for me to visit you there, and I can come right away. I've been there before, so I know the way."

A few seconds later, Jason said, "Dad, Mr. George says you should all come out right away, and Mrs. George says she has plenty of food for brunch for all of us. And Jenny says to tell Julia to bring Buddy out to meet Denny. Oh God, do I need to see you, Dad."

"I can't get there fast enough, Son. I'll see you in a short while. Bye for now." Tom had tears in his eyes.

It was almost noon, so they all loaded into the Toyota and headed downtown to pick up the kids. They were waiting—tossing sticks into the river for Buddy to chase down. While Eric and Tom secured the canoe, Carol related what was happening. Julia was ecstatic, knowing that Jason would reunite with his dad. Thirty minutes later, the Nicholsons and Georges witnessed a tearful and happy reunion of the two men. Carol and Annie were also in tears. After the tears dried, they all enjoyed a happy brunch, although it's doubtful whether Tom or Jason even knew what they were eating.

Walter brought out a bottle of champagne for a celebratory toast after lunch. "A toast," he said "to new and dear friends. I believe we have all made one another happy these last few days. Cheers to Tom and Jason."

"Hear, hear! Well said, Walter," added Eric.

Jason, Eric, and Julia then described how they met, Jason admitting to his weakness at the time in considering suicide. "And I think I can say that Buddy here saved the day for all of us, so I'd like to propose a toast to Buddy. Cheers again!"

Each person got to tell their version of how things were working out, including Jenny, who seemed happiest of all for having found Denny.

"And I thank my hero and best friend, Julia, for that", she added.

"Yay Jenny!" echoed Leah.

***

15. Nicholsons go Riding

On Monday, the Nicholsons and Leah arrived at Horsekey Ranch at 9 a.m. Walter picked out suitable horses for each rider, showed them the basics of saddling, and then gave instructions for riding. They headed north on the George property. The four adults followed the children, with Buddy and Denny dashing back and forth.

Walter commented to Eric, "Jason has more experience than I thought. Besides doing more fencing than I expected in a short time, he even repaired the lighting in my barn. I hope he'll stay around for a while. I can sure use help like that."

As they rode on, Walter pointed out where the pipeline crossed his land. "Why, it's not even buried deep", remarked Eric. "Seems sloppy."

Walter pointed out where the pipeline crossed his land.

"That's right. They laid it on the ground, then plowed dirt over it. That was before Tom took over, which is why we can't move any heavy equipment across it. We can cross it here on this little hill because we put two extra feet of dirt over it. However, Tom assured me they would build a bridge across it now."

Eric then turned to Julia. "Julia, do you recall that question you asked me the day you noticed the tanker leaking oil in the Strait of Georgia? Why don't you ask Mr. George about that now?"

"Oh, yes," she said, turning to Walter. "Back in May my teacher suggested that many First Nations people support the pipeline construction, because many would get jobs working on the pipeline. Do you believe that Mr. George?"

"You've hit on an important question, Julia, and one that I would discuss with your dad. They've already constructed some parts of the pipeline, including this portion on my land, without my initial permission."

Glancing toward Eric, Walter continued. "A few bands in the B.C. interior favour the pipeline because of the jobs issue. I may as well let the cat out of the bag—our band is inviting your whole family as guests at our potlatch next Saturday evening. The following week there is a First Nations Western Conference in Kamloops. We would like to present a united front at the conference. If we can get most bands in British Columbia united against the pipeline, then our lawyers tell us they may get a court injunction to stop its completion. They think this is possible because most of our bands were not consulted before construction started. They just went around offering jobs and took that to be consultation."

"The old *divide and conquer*", replied Eric.

"Yes, so our chief, Chief Byron Tumelta, will bring up this same question with you, Eric, and perhaps ask you for advice on how to respond to those members thinking of potential jobs on the pipeline. But don't feel obligated, as the potlatch invitation is our way of thanking you for already helping us on negotiations with Pacific Western Pipelines."

"We would be honoured to attend the potlatch. This may be a once-in-a-lifetime event for the kids to experience. I'll listen to Chief Tumelta, and if he wishes me to address the band, or the conference next week, I'll do what I can. Meanwhile, I understand there are certain protocols that visitors should follow at a potlatch, so perhaps you could coach us on that."

"Why don't you come back for lunch on Thursday," Annie spoke up. "We can go riding again in the afternoon. Walter can explain the potlatch ceremony, and we can barbeque at our place in the evening."

"Lovely," said Carol. "Consider us in!"

"Yes," Eric concurred. "Now, Walter, tomorrow we planned to get away for the day for more fishing. I think we'll try a pond or lake this time instead of the river. Do you have any recommendations?"

"Sure. If you take the Princeton Highway 97C east, there are quite a few lakes out that way that have beautiful trout in them. One that I like is Englishmen Lake. It's on Kane Valley Road maybe 15 kilometres from the Coquihalla on 97C, then about 12 kilometres southwest on Kane Valley. The lake is only a kilometer long. If you're taking your canoe, paddle over to the west side where there are some lovely deep pools for trout. There must be a dozen other ponds and lakes along that road that you could also try, but Englishmen has never disappointed me for fishing."

"Thanks for the local information. That sounds like the route we should take."

"Then on the way back to town, continue along Kane Valley, where the scenery is stunning. You can't access the Coquihalla from it, but it runs beneath the Coquihalla. You meet up with the Coldwater Road about one kilometre further on. Then you drive back to Merritt on the Coldwater."

Before heading back to their campground, Annie asked Carol, "Do you still want to meet tomorrow evening to plan our strategy for our report?"

"Oh, yes. We'll be back at the campground for dinner. Why don't you meet me there at say, 7 p.m.?"

"Okay."

***

16. Trouble at Englishmen Lake

The next morning, the Nicholsons drove out on Highway 97C, as Walter had suggested. Julia had invited Leah along. With Carol navigating, Eric had no problem finding Englishmen Lake. They noted that someone was already fishing from a small rowboat. With five of them and one canoe, Carol elected to fish from the shore with the two girls, while Eric paddled to the west side with John for the first couple of hours.

"Head back about 11:30, and we'll have lunch together," said Carol. "Then the girls and I have time to go across."

"Good morning," Eric called to the gentleman as they paddled alongside, seeing that he was taking a break for a snack.

"Ah, a beautiful day for trouting, isn't it?" he replied. "Name's Arthur Green. I don't believe we've met before. Are you from around here?"

"No, from Vancouver. We're holidaying around Merritt for two weeks. I'm Eric Nicholson, and my son John here. My wife, Carol, is back along the shore with our daughter and her newfound friend from the Coldwater band."

"I trust you're having a pleasant time?"

"Definitely! We've experienced more events in one week than I see in two months. . . . How's the fishing?"

"Oh, you've come to the right pond. I've often gotten my full quota in this pond, although this is my first time out here this year. You may have noticed, though, that someone has bought up the land around the lake. He's placed private property signs all around the lake, and I see he's almost finished building a rather enormous home here on this side. Can't see that he can keep people off the pond, however, since the road allowance comes right up to the lake on the east side where you just launched."

222

"Does that mean we're trespassing out here then?"

"No way, since the lake and the land along the road is crown land, so he can't stop us from fishing. I chair a fish conservation group around Merritt, the Coldwater Fishers Society. That signage will be reported back to our group when we meet next week. Hopefully this chap doesn't give us any trouble over fishing here."

"You and me both," Eric replied.

At that moment, John said "Wow!"

"Oops, I see your young fellow there hooked a trout while we were talking."

Eric grabbed his net, while calming John down with, "Son, don't jerk your rod too much. Let him take the line a bit, then reel him in, and I'll net him for you."

"He feels big, Dad."

"Looks like a large one, all right. That's it, you're doing fine. He's hooked good, so just reel him in."

A few moments later, John had his catch alongside, and Eric scooped it into his net. "Good, John, looks like at least two pounds. You did well".

"He sure did," said Arthur Green.

The two boats separated a distance for a while, and over the next half an hour, John caught three more, while Eric caught two. Arthur, they noted, also pulled in several trout. It was then that Eric noticed a boat coming off the shore near the new house. He was coming fast with an over-sized motor for fishing. Eric motioned for John to bring his line in. Some 50 metres away, Arthur Green had also pulled in his line. The motorboat roared up between them, and a youthful man called out. "Don't you people know that you're trespassing? This is a private lake now, as we've bought up the surrounding land."

"And who might I be talking to?" replied Eric.

"Name's Murray Giffen, if you need to know. I represent the CEO of the Canadian Petroleum Corporation in Calgary, and we're building a private resort here on this now-private lake, and you must leave."

Arthur Green had listened in and spoke up now. "I don't know where you're from, my friend. You're not from Canada. Otherwise you would know that you cannot claim a lake that's on crown land, just because you bought up land around it. This is a public lake, meaning we have every right to be fishing here. And if you don't mind, that motor of yours has scared the fish away, so please tame it down as you go back."

"I don't think you heard me. You are trespassing, and I want you off the lake. Now! If you're not off in the next half an hour, I get the cops out here to arrest you all." He then opened up his throttle and roared back to the west side.

"Friendly chap, isn't he Arthur? He's already scared the fish off like you said. We may as well leave and address this matter with the authorities in Merritt, as I'm confident that you're correct. I've never heard of anyone owning a public lake either."

"He's a bloody Yank, and has no business talking to us like that," Arthur replied, quite upset. "These millionaires and billionaires come up here thinking they can take over the province with their money."

"Well, we can't settle it right now. I'd like to follow up on this with you later. Why don't we head back to shore and exchange contact information? My son is upset by this, and I'm not thrilled about it myself."

"All right, let's do that. I parked my car and trailer just a few hundred yards down the road from where you are. If you like, we could join forces again on one of the other lakes down the road. There's trout in all of them."

They headed back, and Eric explained what was going on to Carol and the girls. After loading the canoe on the rooftop, they drove 200 metres down the road where Arthur was just packing up. After introductions and exchanging business cards, Arthur suggested going back to Kanes Lake just three or four kilometers back the way they had come.

"Harmon Lake is between them, but it's shallow and more of a busy resort area. Fishing is not as good there. You noticed lots of people on that lake as you drove here."

"Yes, we did and decided not to try fishing there earlier."

Eric followed Arthur to a small launch on Kanes Lake. They fished there for several hours, taking turns with the canoe, while Arthur also shared his row boat with the Nicholsons. John caught a dozen good trout—more than his parents and the girls combined. At 4 p.m., they packed up, as everyone was ready to head back to Merritt. Eric agreed to be a witness for any trial that arose, and Arthur promised to stay in touch by email.

On the drive back to Merritt, Carol remarked, "So Arthur believes they have no right to drive us off that lake?"

"Yes, and I believe he's correct. He mentioned that this has happened on several other lakes in the area, and his group, the Coldwater Fishers Society, has been fund raising and have hired a lawyer to take them to court. There are several billionaires involved from the oil industry, who have no shortage of money and big name lawyers, but Arthur is confident that they are within their rights. One corporation involved is the Canadian Petroleum Corporation. Their society just needs to collect enough money to ensure they can engage in a lengthy trial."

"Isn't that the same corporation that's involved with the pipeline?"

"That's right. CanPet is the main user of the pipeline owned by Tom's company, Pacific Western Pipeline. I don't know how close these two corporations are connected, but they seem to have the federal and Alberta governments supporting them."

"Well, we still caught lots of fish today, and I think everyone had lots of fun."

"And John caught the most fish, and the biggest one again," said Julia.

"He sure did," added Leah. "Thank you Mr. and Mrs. Nicholson for taking me with you. I enjoyed today."

"You are most welcome, Leah. We enjoyed having you along."

They dropped Leah off at her home near to the campground. Then they went back to their trailer, where Eric and Julia cleaned enough trout for them all. Carol started cooking them along with French fries that they picked up at a local takeout.

Annie dropped by with Jenny early that evening, as she and Carol were going out for coffee to discuss their pipeline reports, while Eric took the three children to an early movie. When they got back at 9 p.m., Carol and Annie had just finished their discussion on the impacts of pipelines on First Nations communities.

After Annie left, Carol and Eric went for a brief walk as the sun was setting. "You know," Carol started, "John is becoming skillful in both his fishing and canoeing. Yesterday he caught more trout than the rest of us combined. I gave Annie half the total catch when we got back this evening. Maybe we should think of moving up our planned trip to the NWT?"

"I agree. I've been watching John's canoeing too, and he's about equal to Julia at that age. Let's think about that NWT trip for next summer instead of waiting until 2010 like we had planned."

Just then, Eric received a call on his cell phone from Tom Beasley. "Eric, could I drop by and see you tomorrow morning?

There's something I'd like to discuss with you and to get your advice."

"Of course," Eric replied. "Carol is planning to canoe and fish with the kids in the morning, so I'll hang about here until you arrive."

"Thanks. I'll be there by 9:30."

***

17. Career Decision for Tom

Tom arrived the next morning as Carol and the kids were setting out. Eric had the coffee pot on. "Good morning, Tom".

"Yes, good morning. It's a beautiful day out there."

As he placed coffees on the table, Eric said, "So, what's up?"

"Well, Jason and I have had plenty of discussions this weekend, with lots of catching up ahead."

"I would imagine so."

"My problem is the company wants to close the Kamloops office in September, now that the pipeline problem may be settled for the moment. But they want me to go back to Saudi Arabia to manage their mid-east projects for the next two years, possibly longer. It's a splendid opportunity, with good money, but I can't leave Jason now after just finding him. And I don't think taking him to Saudi and to a total change of culture would help him just now. He needs me, and I'm thinking of pulling my shares in the company and resigning. Besides, I've had second thoughts about the advisability of the pipeline, anyway. I went online and looked at some work you've been doing on climate change research, and that helped solidify my decision. With my engineering background, it's not as if I'd have much trouble getting a fresh job. Even if the pay is less, I need to ensure that Jason gets a fresh start. He's a good kid, and my leaving now would devastate him. He had good high school grades, despite the mess he got into, so if he's interested, he should easily get into a university."

"I think you're making the right decision—for you both," said Eric.

"Do you think you could put in a suitable word for him if he applies to the University of Vancouver?"

"Assuming his grades are as you say. Do you know where his interest lies?"

"It's too early to say. I think he will continue working until January, perhaps study during the winter session. Then he should know what direction he wants to take."

"I suspect he'll want to be in the same city as you, and like you say, he needs your guidance for a while until he regains his confidence. Do you have any job leads yourself yet?"

"No, but I plan to be working on resumes the rest of this week. I don't think I'll have much of a problem. But first I need to submit my resignation to my company. I just needed to speak with someone else about this, and because I sense that you're someone who will understand, perhaps give me more insight. It helps to bare one's soul now and then."

"I understand what you're saying. I sort of do that most days with Carol. She's always been my soul mate."

"I can tell Carol is a wonderful person. . . . You know, that's something else I'll run by you. I met this woman, Janine, in Kamloops two months ago. She's about my age, got over a difficult divorce of two years ago, like myself I guess, and we've gone out together a few times. When I told her about Jason last weekend, she was just about as excited as me. And I know deep down that she was not trying to give me a false impression or anything. That may be another good reason to change careers and settle down more, although we are both taking our time over this. Janine and I have actually had many discussions about possibilities between us, even admitting our own faults. But mostly we've talked about mutual respect for each other, no matter what we decide to do. Neither of us wants to make the same mistakes again. However, re-learning how to date is difficult. You know, it's an unfamiliar world from 25 years ago. Men don't take the lead on everything today."

"Hey, I'm happy for you. You're making several new and major decisions in your life, so I think it's good sense to speak about these things with others you trust. Does Jason know about your recent friend?"

"Oh yes, he was glad for us too. He knows that his mother and I were having marital problems, although much of that was my fault. I was spending too much time on my career, especially travel. Last evening over dinner, Jason jokingly suggested he might have to call Janine Mom, if she and I get more serious about a permanent relationship. I told him it was far too early for Janine and I to think about anything permanent, and I'm sure Janine would prefer that he used her first name."

Eric chuckled and added, "I hope this all works out for the better for the three of you, Tom. You deserve a good break. Let me know later how I might help, as a reference or whatever."

"Thanks, just lending me your ear has been help enough for now. . . . Well, I have to get back and write some letters and resumes, so I hope we'll see you again before you head back to Vancouver."

"You bet. Good luck with your writing today."

***

18. Corporate Deception

That evening at dinner, Carol was delighted to hear about Tom's decision.

"It's best for Jason just now. He seems like a fine young man. I hope he stays on track."

"I'm certain he will. He and his dad have renewed what must have been an excellent relationship."

Julia had been listening and during a break in her parents' discussion said, "Mom, can I tell Dad what I heard today?"

"Why, of course, Julia."

"Leah's dad told her that CanPet had offered full-time jobs only to the Coldwater and Nicola bands. Pacific Western owns the pipeline, but CanPet owns the oil that flows in it. They are hiring for the pipeline construction and maintenance. Some members of the band want to accept the offer. Her dad is interested, so there's a debate going on in the band, and they want to discuss it and have a vote soon. That's the same company, CanPet, that made a similar offer to the Tsleil-Waututh Nation in Vancouver, but they're telling each group they're the only ones getting this offer. That's rather deceptive, isn't it?"

"Yes it is, and it's a psychological ploy to make each band feel they are getting special treatment," replied Eric. "I wonder how many other bands received individual offers like that across British Columbia."

"Yes," Carol interjected, "CanPet has lied about not making individual offers to other First Nations bands. I'm sure we'll find out more about all this from Chief Tumelta Saturday evening during the potlatch."

"Hmm, yes, it should be interesting. And Julia, I may call on you to explain this. You first heard about these offers from

CanPet back in Vancouver; offers that they now claim that only the Coldwater and Nicola bands received."

"Okay. . . . Mom, Dad, Leah invited me to go canoeing with her tomorrow, up the Coldwater River, where we haven't been yet. They have a real birch bark canoe that her dad made. I sure want to try it out. That's okay, isn't it?"

"I don't see why not," replied Eric. "Carol?"

"I think it's a lovely idea Julia. Have you two decided how far upriver you will go? Won't it be difficult paddling up the Coldwater?"

"Well, we won't be paddling up the river. Leah's dad will take us in his truck as far as the Basin Reserve Bridge. That's about 25 kilometres from here she said, and we'll paddle down the river. There are no rapids, and it should be fun. If it's okay, I'd like to bring Buddy with us. He enjoys sitting in the canoe. Leah has a site to show me she says looks just like an old UFO landing site. She says it's just the shape of the land on the west side of the river. When she comes by Thursday morning, we should be able to show you on the map."

***

On Thursday morning, Leah arrived at the Nicholson trailer at 8 o'clock with her dad in tow. Carol and Julia were getting breakfast prepared.

"Mom, Dad, this is Leah, and her dad."

"Hi folks, my name is Jack Holmes. I just thought I'd pop in to meet you, since these two young ladies will be off on a brief adventure."

As Eric shook hands with Jack, he said, "I'm glad to meet you. This is my wife, Carol, our daughter, Julia, and our son, John.

"Leah tells me you've gotten to know Walter George and his family."

"Yes. In fact, we're going to Walter and Annie's ranch this afternoon to do some riding. Do you know them?"

"Oh, for sure. Walter and I went to school together, used to play on the same Lacrosse teams growing up. We were both attackers on the same team for several years. We often still get together at various events, sometimes fish together when Walter's not busy with his trail guiding. They're splendid people and well respected in our community."

Carol spoke up while shaking hands with Jack. "It's a pleasure to meet you, Jack. We never thought we'd make so many friends here in Merritt."

"And I hear you're all invited to the potlatch tomorrow evening. We've often discussed in Council how we need to get to know folks from non-Native backgrounds and integrate more, you know."

"We sure find Coldwater and Nicola people to be friendly," said Eric.

"I must apologize, Jack," said Carol. "We're not being hospitable. Why don't you and Leah join us for breakfast? We are just ready to sit down."

"I had breakfast just an hour ago, but a piece of toast and a coffee would be fine."

"Unfortunately there's little room in this travel trailer, but it's so nice outside this morning. Why don't we sit at the picnic table there?"

While Eric was pouring coffee, Carol and Julia put breakfast on the table outside. Carol said, "We're glad you dropped by, Jack. What kind of paddling can the girls expect on the Coldwater today?"

"The lower part of the Coldwater is just a slow, meandering river. There are a few rough spots or minor rapids on straight stretches, but nothing more than what's just outside here. Leah's a strong paddler too, been canoeing since she was five or six. And there's no way they can get in trouble on the river unless they went up 30 kilometres. There it's rougher, where the river comes out of the mountains."

Leah spoke up and said, "Dad is driving us as far as the Basin Reserve Bridge, about 25 kilometres from here. I wanted to show Julia the old UFO site, or that's what we've always called it. It's just a few kilometers down from the bridge."

"Well then," Eric started, "Julia is a good paddler herself, as she's been in canoes just about as long as Leah. It's one of her favourite activities. They should be fine together."

"Even taking their time, they'd only be three or four hours coming back to here."

They packed a light lunch, and Julia insisted they take along a fishing rod …..in case we get starving," she said.

Eric brought out his laptop, and bringing up Google Earth, Leah showed the adults the Basin Reserve Bridge, then the site of the UFO landing.

"I see what you mean by the Coldwater meandering in this lower section."

Half an hour later, Julia and Buddy hopped into the back cab of the pickup, while Leah got in front with her dad.

John called out just before they drove off, "You be careful Julia".

"I will", she replied.

***

Eric, Carol, and John then went shopping that morning to find some small gifts to bring to the Georges before leaving for home on Sunday. Julia had asked her mother to pick up something for Jenny. Carol chose a bracelet which matched Jenny's locket and chain, while John picked out a board game for William. Carol found an embroidered apron for Annie, for she knew Annie liked to cook, and Eric bought a brand of Scotch whisky that he knew Walter liked. Then they headed out to the Georges for lunch.

During lunch, Carol and Annie announced that they had agreed to collaborate on a report to the Coldwater and Nicola bands on how the pipeline was affecting First Nations. A later step might be to publish the report in book form. Walter and Eric toasted the women on their endeavour and hoped it would signal more collaboration.

They were just ready to mount their horses for the afternoon ride when Eric's phone rang. He recognized Julia's number. "Hi Julia, how's your trip going?" he asked.

***

19. Investigation of Pipeline Break

While driving southwest on Coldwater Road, Jack pointed out where there was a reported oil spill from a broken pipeline on Tuesday, just inside the trees on the east side of the river. "The spill isn't visible from the road," he said.

"How much oil was spilled?" asked Julia.

"The company claims there were less than 100 litres spilled before they shut down the pipeline. They won't let any of us on the property, which is Coldwater Band lands, because they say they're using some dangerous chemicals in the clean-up, and they don't want any accidents among the public. Leah here thinks they may not be telling the entire truth about the spill. I don't buy the dangerous chemicals part, if their own people are using it for clean-up; but otherwise, their explanation sounds reasonable to me."

Leah added, "The spill is close to the river. If it seeps into the river, it could kill plenty of salmon."

"That reminds me, you might see the spill when you canoe back down the river." A few moments later, Jack added, "Hmm, I don't suppose that's the reason for this trip, is it?"

"Well, it's an extra reason."

"Okay, but you be real careful, and if the oil folks tell you to stay off the land there, you listen, right?"

"Of course, Dad", and Leah couldn't help smiling a little, Julia noted.

A few minutes later, they turned off on Paul's Basin Reserve Road, and shortly after, they stopped at the bridge over the Coldwater River. Jack helped them lift the canoe onto the river, and said, "Well, you're on your own from here. Keep track of your location, and you both have cells, so if you run into trouble at all, call me or Mr. Nicholson. It shouldn't be too hard for you to find Merritt again, as long as you stay on the river." The girls giggled at that.

Jack winked and said, "Now, if you do just happen to get a few photos of the oil spill, I'm sure it would interest the band at the potlatch. And be careful of rocks. This canoe is light, manoeuvrable, and swift, but easier to damage than Julia's aluminum one.

"We'll be careful. Thanks Dad. See you this evening."

As they got into the canoe, Julia called, "Buddy, come!" Buddy jumped into the canoe and sat at the bow as if he was riding shotgun.

As they paddled, Julia said, "Am I guessing wrong that the oil spill is your principal reason for this trip?"

"Yeah, well . . . It was tempting for Dad to accept the oil company offer and one of their positions. He hasn't agreed yet, but they told him he might get a permanent job and more training with the company, Canadian Petroleum Corporation. But on Tuesday, we heard about the pipeline break south of Merritt near that UFO site. I think it's strange that they wouldn't let band members see the oil spill, and yet they claim the spill was only 100 litres, which is not much to clean up. If it's more than that, and if it's close to the river, then we would worry about pollution, since many in our band, including our family, depend on fishing for our living."

"You're suspicious about what the company is claiming?"

"You bet. The band seems satisfied with the company explanation, but I'm not so sure we can trust them."

"So, we can get in by the back door to see the spill from the river, right?"

"Yeah. I know the area well, since it's part of the Coldwater Band lands. . . . You don't mind, do you?"

"Heck, a little excitement will be fun. If anyone sees us, we can just pretend we know nothing about the spill, or don't know where it is, anyway. Besides, their explanation sounds suspicious to me too."

The two girls concentrated on their paddling for a few minutes. They were both experienced and coordinated well, so Julia remarked, "Wow, this canoe sure travels well."

After about six kilometres, Leah said, "Hey, our UFO site is just up ahead on the west side. Why don't we beach there and have lunch?"

"Excellent idea!"

They climbed up the river bank, and Leah pointed out a near-circular area of about 50 metres diameter that appeared to be burnt.

"Nothing ever grows on that spot," Leah said, "and it's been like that for years, so us kids called it a UFO landing site."

Julia scuffed the ground with her foot. "It looks like it's burnt. I wonder why nothing ever grows again. Burning grass puts nitrogen back in the soil, and it grows even greener after that."

"I guess it burns the soil too deep or something. We can never get cell phone coverage anywhere near this site too. It might be some strange radiation or something. Anyway, there are several cut tree stumps over there where we can sit and snack."

"We're close to the oil spill here, aren't we?"

"Yes, just around the next bend, about a half kilometre. There are two small oxbow ponds on the opposite side of the river. We could stop there, maybe have a look-see. Wadda-you-say?"

"Of course! I want to see it too."

"There are lines of trees along the oxbows, so we should be able to sneak up there and see what's happening with no one seeing us."

They packed up their garbage, got back in the canoe, and

paddled less than half a kilometre to the next bend and beached on the southeast side. They walked up to the oxbow, then stared in shock at a thick layer of oil on it. Beyond, they could see a veritable mess of oil all over the land for several hundred metres. Buddy, being a golden retriever, was all set to jump into the oxbow cutoff, but stopped, took one sniff, then turned away.

R1920-(6c) UFO landing site, oxbow pond, and pipeline break.
(From Google-Earth).

"My gosh, there's more than 100 litres of oil spilled here, that's for sure," whispered Julia. "There must be a couple of dozen people working on the clean-up. And I see half a dozen dump trucks lined up there too, to take away contaminated soil, I suppose."

"No kidding. My instinct was right. They're not telling the band the whole truth."

Julia took some photos with her cell phone. They backtracked to the oxbow and took more photos there.

"Why couldn't CanPet be honest about it, and just tell the public that it's a serious oil spill?" Julia asked.

"Because they don't want any bad press just now. That could kill the pipeline proposal as far as band approval goes right there. But if that oil gets into the Coldwater, it might be goodbye to fish and fishing."

"These oxbow ponds could be the saving grace there if they can keep the oil from spreading further."

"What should we do, Julia?"

"We need to check to see if they alerted the authorities about this yet."

"This will end any debate about pipeline jobs around here. Who should we report this to?" asked Leah.

"Environment Canada perhaps. I'm not certain, but Dad will know. Let's paddle on a way, and when we have cell coverage I'll call Dad and text these photos to him. He'll know who to contact."

They paddled around the next bend, then had an open stretch of river for almost two kilometres. As they went by the spill on a large open area, they noted a hayfield covered in oil, so Julia took more photos. The oil was seeping down close to the river. They noticed the crews working on the clean-up again, and a few looked up and pointed at them paddling by, but nobody appeared too concerned. At that point, they came on some mild rapids where the flow was faster, so the next kilometre went by fast.

"They will think we're just two unconcerned kids," said Leah.

Once out of sight, they pulled ashore once more and Julia phoned her dad. Eric answered. "Hi Julia, how's your trip going?" he asked.

"Great," she replied, "but guess what. That oil spill is no mere 100 litres. It's a terrible mess, and very close to the river.

I'll text you some photos as soon as we hang up. Who should we contact about this?"

"Let me go over the photos first," he replied. "Then I'll call you back."

Julia sent about half a dozen of the best photos. Then they waited. Eric called back in less than ten minutes.

"Julia. That is a serious oil spill. I'll alert Environment Canada right away, their Kamloops office, and get them to look into it straightaway. Good work, girls! I hope you're on the way back now?"

"Yes, Leah says it's less than three hours back from here, and we don't plan to stop anywhere else just now."

After Eric contacted Environment Canada, the Georges and Nicholsons continued their ride around the perimeter of the Horsekey Ranch. Eric explained what Julia and Leah had uncovered and showed them her photos.

"The band will be interested in this", said Walter. This is what Chief Tumelta needs to convince most of the band to vote against the new pipeline. Unfortunately, the government may well find some excuse to approve the pipeline, regardless. But it's important for the band to have one voice on this."

As they were riding, they reviewed all that had happened in the past two weeks, and Carol marveled at how everything was coming together.

"I'm not so surprised at that," said Walter. "That young lady of yours is something else, the way she digs at clues and gets the right answers. She has sure impressed Annie and I."

"And do you know," Annie interjected, "that Jenny doesn't stop talking about Julia? Julia is her hero, and she wants to be just like her. We think she's wonderful, and an outstanding role model for Jenny."

"Well," said Carol, "we think you folk are wonderful too."

"Speaking of which," added Walter, "why don't you call Julia back and suggest that she and Leah both come out for the barbeque? I'm sure one of us could go pick them up."

"Okay, I'll do that", and Eric called Julia again. Both Julia and Leah were ecstatic about coming out, for Julia felt bad about not seeing Jenny. Leah had only to call her dad or mom to okay it. Eric said he would pick them up in about one hour.

They had all thoroughly enjoyed the ride, especially the three children. Once they arrived back at the ranch in mid-afternoon, Eric excused himself to pick up Julia and Leah. He was back in 90 minutes. Jenny rushed out to greet her hero and Leah.

Annie and Carol were inside making salads and a dessert, while Walter was getting the barbeque ready. He said, "Hello Leah. How are your mom and dad?"

"Fine, thank you, and thank you for inviting us out."

"Oh, any time."

"Grab a beer from the cooler there, Eric," Walter suggested.

While relaxing, Eric asked Walter again about any protocols concerning the potlatch that would be useful to know.

"Well," Walter started, "We have potlatches on the occasion of births, deaths, adoptions, weddings, and other major events. Non-band members rarely attend these except by invitation, and you and your family have a special invitation. All you need to know is not to sit in the front row, which we reserve for the elders, unless the Chief asks you to be up front. The major event this time is a preparation for the First Nations Western Conference in Kamloops next week, where they'll be discussing the pros and cons of this new pipeline. Our Chief wanted to argue against it, but some members were hanging back. I agree with Chief Tumelta on this issue, despite the new arrangement I have with Pacific Western Pipeline now, after they forced the first one on me. But this news about the pipeline break and a major spill will turn the tide, at least among the Coldwater and Nicola bands."

"Don't feel bad about your agreement last week with Tom Beasley," Eric said. He then related how Tom Beasley had told him this week he was resigning from Pacific Western Pipeline.

"Tom's company wanted to close the Kamloops office and have Tom take over their operations in the Middle East, based out of Saudi Arabia. But Tom wants to spend more time with Jason, and he's also been having second thoughts about the pipeline and the possible environmental risks. He hopes to find an engineering position around Kamloops; otherwise, he'll try Vancouver."

"Now that's interesting, because our band is considering hiring an experienced engineer to advise them on these issues, and other projects, and they would like to get someone with experience like Tom has. Would Tom be interested in that?"

"I'm sure he would, depending on the details, and as long as his current job does not put him in a legal conflict of interest, having insider information and all that entails."

"Let's see what comes up tomorrow evening, and we can let Tom know later what possibility might be open to him."

Carol later remarked, "We had such a good time riding and talking today, that I didn't have time to worry about getting aches from riding, so I don't feel any pain at all today."

"By gosh, you're right," agreed Eric. "I feel fine too, where I was sore all evening the last time."

"You're becoming rodeo material already," joked Annie. "Come on in and freshen up before we start the barbeque. Take a shower if you wish."

***

20. Potlatch

On Saturday morning, Eric received a call back from the Environment Canada office in Kamloops.

"Dr. Nicholson, this is Jim Thomson from Environment Canada test labs in Kamloops. I thought I would follow up with you on the oil spill you, or your daughter, reported yesterday."

"Yes, I'm very interested, because we are meeting with the Coldwater and Nicola bands this evening, and they need to be informed. And it was my daughter and her friend from the Coldwater Band who discovered what appears to be a deception by Canadian Petroleum."

"Well, to start, the revised estimate of the spill is closer to 10,000 litres. CanPet is only required initially to report a spill, which they did. If no information on the amount is available, since these are often in remote areas, then it's recorded as the minimum 100 litres. However, as soon as they reach a site, then they must update the volume of the spill. They neglected to do that in this case, presumably because they are still negotiating with bands to approve the pipeline. They will be fined for that oversight. You can convey that information, 10,000 litres, to the band as the nearest estimate. If they require further confirmation, please have them call me. I'll text you my contact information as soon as we hang up."

"The band will appreciate this, as the company denied them entry to the spill site, even though it is Coldwater Band land."

"That's another count against CanPet. They cannot deny access to the band on their own lands."

"Well, thank you, Jim, for this information."

"You're most welcome". Thank *you* for reporting it."

"Bye for now."

Arriving at the Potlatch, Chief Byron Tumelta, in full headdress, greeted them warmly. "Dr. Nicholson, you honour us by coming to our ceremony this evening. I've heard much about you and your family, especially this young lady, Julia. Welcome to all of you. Please sit up front with the elders as our honoured guests. The ceremony will begin shortly."

Potlatch similar to Coldwater/Nicola Bands - Peace Dance performed at Bill Cranmer's 1983 Potlatch in Alert Bay, BC. Photo by permission from Vickie Jensen.

Julia and John were impressed with the formality and costumes of the dancers and drummers that followed. An elder then addressed the band. He spoke eloquently about the environment around the Nicola Valley, how the great creator had formed the valley for the Coldwater and Nicola Bands, and how it was their responsibility to look after the valley and Mother Earth.

Chief Tumelta then took over. He first thanked the Elder for his wise words, and then acknowledged the Nicholson family as their special guests.

He then brought up the pipeline, saying "last week I attended a protest against the pipeline in Burnaby, along with members from many bands in southern B.C. While we were there, a ship ran aground and spilled some of its cargo of oil. It was a small spill and easily cleaned up. However, it served as a warning to us if the pipeline is completed, about the dangers of increased tanker and other ship traffic in the Strait of Georgia or beyond until a tanker gets into the Pacific Ocean. When I returned here last weekend, I heard of a pipeline break near the Alberta-B.C. border. It was also reported as a small spill, again easily cleaned up. The Creator is getting anxious and is warning us about more disasters to follow if this new pipeline goes through."

"I know that some of you believe we should approve the pipeline, as there will be many jobs available during the construction. But those jobs are short term, and may not last more than a year. What then? Once the pipeline is completed, the only jobs available will be for trained engineers and technicians. Few of us will be trained for or offered those jobs. ... I now invite anyone present to make comments or ask questions."

Several members put up their hands. Chief Tumelta motioned one member to come forward to address the band at the microphone.

"Chief, I am James Petard from the Lower Nicola band. Recently a manager from the Canadian Petroleum Corporation in Calgary contacted several of us. They own the oil being shipped through the pipeline. He spoke about offering training for full-time jobs after they complete the pipeline. He said that his company is only offering these positions to members of the Coldwater-Nicola Bands, but if we don't take advantage of it now, the offers will go to another band."

Chief Tumelta responded. "I'm surprised that this gentleman did not approach me first as your elected chief. Regardless, that's a good point, if such is the case." . . . "A few minutes ago I acknowledged the Nicholson family, visiting from Vancouver, as our special guests. Some of you know that Mr. Nicholson, actually *Dr.* Nicholson, is an expert on climate change and environmental issues. I would like to ask him if he has any words to respond to this issue. . . . Dr. Nicholson, please do not feel pressured to respond, but you would be more than welcome to share your views."

Eric stood up and motioned to Julia and Leah to join him at the microphone. Julia was not nervous, since her dad had forewarned her. Taking the microphone first, Eric started with "Chief Tumelta, honoured Elders, and members of the Coldwater and Nicola Bands. First, let me say how pleased my family and I are to be guests at your Potlatch. It is a unique opportunity for my two children, especially Julia here, because a few months ago she made new friends with the Burrard Indian Band of the Tsleil-Waututh Nation in the Vancouver area. Then on Wednesday, while she was fishing with her mom and brother, she met this young lady here, Leah Holmes, from your Coldwater Band. Julia learned something of interest from both these two sources. Then, just yesterday, she and Leah learned something even more important to this group while they were canoeing on the Coldwater River. I will let Julia and Leah recount their findings now. Julia?"

"Thank you, Dad," . . . a pause, and the audience laughed. "Yes, I heard about the offer from the Canadian Petroleum

Corporation, that job training would be provided, but only to the Coldwater-Nicola Bands after the pipeline went operational. But a few months ago, I heard the same story from my friend who is a member of the Tsleil-Waututh Nation near Burnaby." There were murmurs from the whole audience at this point. Julia continued. "I wondered how many other bands have received this same unique offer?"

Chief Tumelta cut in at this point. "So, what you are saying is that this offer from CanPet is not as unique as they are letting on?"

"That would seem to be the case."

The audience absorbed this for a moment; then Chief Tumelta said, "Your dad suggested something else that you and Leah learned yesterday. Something important?"

"Yes, but it was Leah who suspected this. She convinced me to go investigate it with her. Leah, would you like to tell them about it?" She passed the portable microphone to Leah.

"Well, I heard about the pipeline oil spill on Tuesday. The company said that the spill was only 100 litres, and they denied band people access to see the spill for themselves, even though it occurred on Coldwater Band lands. I was not happy about that, and suspected something was wrong, so I asked my new friend, Julia to go with me to investigate. Dad drove us with our canoe up as far as the Basin Reserve Bridge, on the excuse (sorry, Dad–*more laughter*) that I wanted to show Julia the old UFO landing site as us kids call it. We stopped at the UFO site, but then headed to our main aim, which was the pipeline oil spill a short way downstream."

"Yes, go on," Chief Tumelta encouraged. "What did you see there?"

"It was shocking, with spilled oil spreading over a large area. It was draining downhill towards the river, which was only about 300 meters away. There are several oxbow cut-offs at that location, which are within 50 meters of the river, and those were covered in layers of oil."

Following a few gasps from the audience, the chief asked "I understand you have photos to show of this?"

"Yes, Julia took several photos, and she can project them on the screen if you wish."

"Please do, Julia."

Julia inserted her camera card into the laptop provided and explained each of the photos. Chief Tumelta expressed shock and dismay at the mess, even though CanPet employees were doing their best to clean it up.

Julia added, "We told my Dad, who alerted Environment Canada yesterday, and they investigated it immediately. This morning they phoned Dad and told him that the spill was about 10,000 litres."

"The company knew this, and still neglected to amend their report of the spill as only 100 litres?"

"Well, that is standard practice until they get to a site themselves and estimate the total damage."

"But they still did not report the actual amount immediately?"

"I guess not", said Julia.

James Petard, who had earlier mentioned the offer of company jobs, and had encouraged band members to vote in favour of the pipeline, raised his hand again to speak.

"Yes James, you have something to add?"

"This is all new to me, and we must all thank the two young ladies, Leah and Julia, for their information. And given that the CanPet representative was not honest with us, twice now, I am withdrawing my support for accepting the pipeline offer."

Several other members chimed in with "that goes for me too".

"Are there any other comments on this issue?" . . . "I believe that we should put this whole matter to a vote now. Would all adults over 18 please line up at the table, pick up a ballot, and check off Yes or No to the pipeline approval. This does not stop any of you from accepting temporary employment with the company, but you should know of their deception. Could I have our vote counters at this end of the table please, to count the ballots. While we wait for the result, take a break once you've completed your vote, and refreshments are at the other end of the room. We'll reconvene as soon as the count is complete."

While the Nicholsons joined the others at the refreshments table, many band members stopped to thank Julia. Chief Tumelta approached Eric and said, "Dr. Nicholson, it is very important for us that you are here this evening, especially with your daughter Julia and her friend Leah."

"You're most welcome. We've attended rallies against the pipeline in Vancouver ourselves. The threat of a pipeline or tanker spill is critical. Besides, the new pipeline is primarily to ship heavy dirty oil from Alberta Oil Sands to refineries in Asia. We might be more open to refined oil products, but the producers do not want to build expensive refineries."

"Why won't they build new refineries, Dr. Nicholson?"

"I believe the energy industry is seeing the writing on the wall for fossil fuels. We must make a rapid shift away from fossil fuels, and it has already started to happen, albeit too slowly. The Tesla Roadster all-electric car is just coming out this year, for example, and full retail production of electric cars can't be more than a few years away."

"So the oil companies don't want to build billion-dollar refineries that could be obsolete in a few years?"

"Something like that, although we'll still need gasoline- and diesel-powered vehicles for some years to come yet, until electric or even hydrogen-powered vehicles prove their worth."

"On another related point, Walter George told me last week that you might require someone to address the overall question of global warming impacts. Is that correct?"

"Ah, you anticipated my next question. Would you be willing to come to Kamloops next week and address our First Nations Western Conference on that topic? I have already checked with the organizers, and they would be very pleased to have someone of your expertise to address the whole conference. They will pay whatever your current rate is, plus all your expenses. I understand that you are returning to Vancouver tomorrow, and it's unfair to ask you to turn around and come back to Kamloops, but you would not need to be there until Wednesday."

"First, I'm delighted that you ask, but second, other than minimal expenses, I do not need any other fee, as that is my job, my mission, to address groups like yours. And flying from Vancouver to Kamloops on Tuesday evening would not be any problem. Consider it done."

"Wonderful. Our secretary will call you Monday and arrange your travel. I have a list of questions on global warming and its impacts here that the conference would like you to address." He passed a list to Eric.

After glancing at the list, Eric replied "this would be no problem at all."

"There is one other matter on which I would like your opinion. We need to hire an engineering expert who could advise the Band on how climate change and new constructions like the pipeline will affect us. There are also water and sewage problems at some bands for example. I understand that you and Walter have good rapport with this Tom Beasley, the engineer from Pacific Western Pipelines. Walter told me today that Mr. Beasley is resigning from the pipeline company. Do you think a position with the band might interest him?"

"I'm almost certain that he would be interested, depending on salary and benefits. I don't know whether his current job might place him in a legal conflict of interest, with having insider information on Pacific Western and CanPet. I cannot speak for him on that."

"Then could you ask him to get in touch with me? Here is my card, and one for Mr. Beasley."

"I will try to contact him before we leave for Vancouver tomorrow."

"Good, good. Now, I see that our ballot counters appear ready to report, so I need to get back to the microphone. Then our banquet gets going. I hope you and your family don't mind eating late like this."

"We're looking forward to it, and to the results of your ballot."

Chief Tumelta went back to the microphone, picked up the count, then addressed the audience again. "Ladies and gentlemen. The results of our ballot are: against the pipeline approval, 275, and only 5 for. I believe that settles that debate. Now, it is time for our banquet. Dinner will be served buffet style on either side of the buffet tables over here. I will ask our elders to go first, then our honoured guests with their new First Nations friends, the Georges and the Holmes."

***

On Sunday morning, Eric called Tom Beasley's cell phone. Tom answered immediately. "Good morning Tom, Eric here. Carol and I wanted to check with you before we return to Vancouver today. How are you and Jason?"

"We're all fine. I put in my resignation letter. The company understands my position regarding Jason. I've also submitted applications to five companies looking for an engineer in the Kamloops area."

"Would you be interested in a sixth position?"

"For sure. Do you have a specific suggestion?"

"Yes, the Nicola Tribal Association needs an engineer, one with experience to advise on various business ventures, the impacts of environmental issues, water and sewage issues in the various bands, and pipeline impacts in particular. Chief Tumelta asked me to mention this to you. If you're interested, I have the Chief's business card for you."

"Janine and I are back here in Merritt for the weekend to see Jason. We could drop over in an hour?"

"Great. We'd love to meet Janine and see Jason again before we leave for home."

Eric and Carol were delighted to meet Tom, Janine, and Jason. Tom was interested in the potential job offer from Chief Tumelta and planned to meet with him the following day.

The Nicholsons were packed and ready to head home, following a happy and eventful two-week holiday. Both the George and Holmes families dropped by to say farewell and to wish them a happy journey. Jenny was teary-eyed when she hugged Julia and made her promise to come visit soon. Julia said she would also bring Buddy back to see Denny. Both Leah and Julia also shed a tear and promised to stay in touch.

Their friendship was to become a great strength for both later.

Walter and Jack shook hands with Eric and thanked him. Walter added, "We'll be seeing you in Kamloops in a few days for the First Nations Western Conference."

***

21. First Nations Western Conference

The Nicholsons arrived home without incident later that day. Annie and Carol had planned to continue work on their 'pipeline impacts' report by email, and Annie accepted Carol's invitation to come to Vancouver in October to complete it. This resulted in the entire family being invited, so they agreed to work around the Thanksgiving weekend so that the children could come along and not miss too much school.

**

The following Thursday, Eric flew to Kamloops to address the First Nations Western Conference. He was pleasantly surprised to see Tom attending the conference, and to learn that Tom had accepted the job offer with the Nicola Tribal Association.

Eric was elated on hearing that Tom and Janine were engaged and planned to marry in December. Tom asked him: "Do you think you and Carol could come out to Kamloops for the wedding?"

"No way would we miss that," Eric replied.

"Jason agreed to be my best man," Tom added, "and he's decided to start studies at the Nicola Valley Institute of Technology this September. He chose environmental and science courses that would be transferrable to any university once he found his true niche."

Following his introduction to the conference, Eric summarized climate change science, and his thoughts on the impacts—especially on coastal British Columbia—and the pipeline controversy.

All bands pledged opposition to the pipeline, unless strict environmental conditions could be met. The Coldwater-Nicola Band Council kept Eric on a small retainer to help Tom develop those conditions.

Members of the Tsleil-Waututh Nation from the coast expressed their concern about federal government talk of increased tanker traffic, which would sail through Burrard Inlet and into the Strait of Georgia and the Salish Sea. Chief Curtis George addressed the gathering. "We are the Tsleil-Waututh First Nation, the People of the Inlet. We have lived in and along our inlet for probably thousands of years, since the Creator transformed the Wolf into that first Tsleil-Waututh, and made the Wolf responsible for this land. Our nation has always depended on the coastal waters for food. Our elders used to say: 'When the tide went out, the table was set.' We have always been here, and we always will be here. Our people are here to care for our land and water. It is our obligation and birthright to be the caretakers and protectors of our inlet. There is no value for us in seeing five to ten times more oil tankers in this inlet. A single accident can ruin our livelihood for a long time."

Following his address, Chief George asked Eric if he could come and explain global warming to his band, and provide his view on the proposed tanker traffic. They agreed on a meeting date for late September.

***

On his return to Vancouver, Eric described the concerns of First Nations bands to Carol, as it had a bearing on the pipeline impacts report that she and Annie George were completing.

Julia listened to their discussion, including the concerns of the Tsleil-Waututh Nation. She asked her dad about the legal implications, and whether a court case would stop the pipeline and the increased tanker traffic that would come with it.

"It's too early to say, Julia," said Eric. "A lot will depend on the pressure that Alberta and Fort McMurray corporations can exert on the provincial and federal governments, and how that affects the court hearings. Are your classes discussing the legal aspects in school?"

"No, but I'm interested in that. I'd like to find out more about it, but a lot of the legal stuff goes over my head."

"Maybe you'll wind up studying environmental law when you go to university in a few years' time. The Law Department at the university is planning a law careers display during the last week of August. Would you like to see what they offer and maybe ask questions?"

"Yes, I would like that."

***

Julia did attend the law careers display that August with her dad, and came home very motivated to study law later.

Her dad advised her: "plenty of time to think about that Julia, but it is wise to develop your career options early. Just study well and keep your options open."

***

22. Oil Tanker Disaster

By mid-September, the Nicholsons were back to their regular family routine in Vancouver. Julia and John were in school, Eric was teaching his climate courses again at UVan, and Carol was back at her job as senior meteorologist and shift supervisor at Environment Canada, Vancouver. Following her night shift one Monday morning, she was home in time to have breakfast with the family.

"How is the weather for this week?" asked Eric.

"Well, there's a low pressure system driving up the coast of Washington today, should have rain this afternoon and evening. It's bringing a lot of warm moist air from the south, so I'd expect fog to form over the colder coastal waters of B.C."

"Oh, no," spoke up Julia. "That old low will ruin our class picnic planned for tomorrow."

"Will the weather clear after it moves through?" asked Eric.

"For a short while, but we expect the storm will get a new surge of energy just as it moves by. We should get more weather from this storm yet."

"Oh?"

"I expect the low will stall for 12-24 hours over the Strait of Georgia, then intensify as more energy pours into it from the south. Then, when it moves off to the northeast, strong westerly winds will develop behind it. That will mean stronger north westerlies in the Strait of Juan de Fuca from the channeling that often occurs there."

". . . Which should then clear out the fog?"

"If the winds are powerful enough, the fog will lift into low status and fog patches."

"So the marine forecast will have fog, lifting with strong north westerlies developing behind it?"

"Exactly!"

"Okay, I need to drop the kids off at school, and then get myself in for my class this morning, while you need to get some rest."

"Right! So, see you about five?"

"Yes. Have a good sleep. Julia, John, let's get going. Bye dear."

***

At 10:30 a.m. the following morning, the Panamanian-registered Aframax oil tanker, *Arribamax*, cast off from Burnaby oil terminal, bound for the Philippines. She had a full load of 100,000 metric tonnes of Fort McMurray heavy crude oil, and a crew of 22. The mandatory Canadian pilot was in the wheelhouse directing the ship's course until they were past the city of Victoria.

An Afromax tanker similar to the Arribamax *in Cowichan Bay, BC, with freefall lifeboat at the rear. (Photo: G.Strong)*

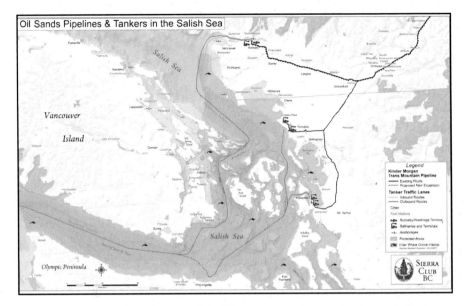

BC end of Pacific Western Pipeline, and outbound/inbound tanker routes from/to Burnaby and the Strait of Georgia – Salish Sea - Strait of Juan de Fuca (with permission from Sierra Club).

Winds were light, as was ship traffic, allowing them to maintain a steady speed of 14 knots as they turned south, and later southeast over the Strait of Georgia. The early marine forecast suggested clearing weather as a low over Vancouver Island moved onto the mainland north of Vancouver. Southwest winds of ten knots would persist during daylight hours, with fog patches around Haro Strait. Widespread fog was expected in the Strait of Juan de Fuca, with visibility less than one kilometer. Winds would shift and increase to northwest 20-25 knots by evening with increasing visibilities. However, there was a warning of gale force winds of 35-45 knots after midnight.

"The stronger winds result from the channeling of winds in the Juan de Fuca after a weather system moves through," said Captain Ross Jones in answer to his chief mate's enquiry about the wind warning. "We should be just about through the strait by midnight, about the time the winds strengthen. How are our electronic systems behaving?"

"Communications reports all systems go," replied the chief, "although he mentioned that our secondary radar is a little wonky, something to do with its rotation, same problem as last crossing."

"Didn't we have that in for maintenance? Oh well, I'm sure it won't be a serious problem."

After sailing southeast across the Strait of Georgia, the *Arribamax* turned southwest into Boundary Pass about 14:00. They came across fog patches as they turned south into Haro Strait at 16:30. The pilot slowed the ship to ten knots here, as they were crossing the path of scheduled ferries between Sidney and the San Juan Islands. The fog thickened as they progressed south through Haro Strait, but winds were only five knots from the southwest. As they rounded Chatham Island just east of Victoria, visibility dropped to under half a kilometre, even as the wind picked up to 12 knots. The pilot slowed *Arribamax* to under five knots as they turned southwest towards the Strait of Juan de Fuca. It was 18:15 and time for their pilot to depart.

"This is where I'll be leaving you, Captain Jones, as I hear my tug coming along with its foghorn. You should check on any update to that wind warning, as things are getting choppy here, despite the fog."

"Yes, our communications officer is checking on that right now before we pick up speed again. There's your tug alongside now, so I thank you for guiding us this far. We shouldn't have any trouble getting through the strait now, even if winds pick up early."

"Have a safe voyage then, Captain Jones," the pilot spoke one last time by VHF radio once he was aboard the tug.

The sun was setting at 19:15 as the *Arribamax* got underway again. The ship's communications officer brought the latest weather report to Captain Jones. "Visibility is improving Sir, up to one kilometre now, but winds are increasing. The afternoon forecast suggested gale force winds of 50-60 knots developing over the next couple of hours."

"So much for a quiet sailing," he noted to his chief mate. "We need to have anything loose on deck battened down. Have a check done right away, please. I'll warn the rest of our crew to stay off open decks."

An hour later, at 20:30, the chief mate told the captain they were coming up near the Race Rocks, for this was where they would turn northwest into the Strait of Juan de Fuca for about 100 kilometres, until they reached the open Pacific Ocean.

At 20:35, the chief mate announced, "Adjusting our heading to two-nine-zero degrees now, Sir."

The communications officer came by with the latest weather advisory. "They now expect winds of 70-90 knots to develop over the Strait, Sir."

"Should be safe for the moment. What's the current wind speed, Chief?"

"Wind speed is . . . wow, 60 knots, gusting to 80, from two-five-five degrees, Sir, right on our port bow."

"Hmm, and I see low stratus clouds moving across our path just up ahead," replied Captain Jones. Before the chief mate could answer, a violent wind and high waves struck *Arribamax* on the port bow, while visibility dropped again to less than 800 metres. The large tanker veered by almost 20 degrees to starboard as they neared the top of 20-foot waves, and the chief mate had to adjust course quickly. "Chief, I think we'll need two extra lookouts up here on the bridge."

At that moment, the wind increased suddenly to over 100 knots, and the heavily laden *Arribamax* laboured. The bridge monitors all flickered for a few moments. The bridge crew heard a loud grinding noise from above. "What was that?" asked the chief.

In response, the communications operator yelled out, "Sir, we've just lost both our radar and radio contact!"

"What's with the radar?" shouted Captain Jones.

"One moment, Captain," responded the communications operator. Ten seconds later, he replied, "Captain, somehow that powerful gust did something to the radar, stripped its gears or something. And we've also lost radio contact along with the radar. Possibly an electronic short took them both out."

"What about our secondary radar?"

"No use. It's gone out too."

"Chief, get those extra lookouts here on the double."

The chief mate replied, "Sir, our auto pilot is also unserviceable!"

This was just the start of a terrifying series of events for the *Arribamax*. Captain Jones ordered the engine room to reduce speed to five knots. The *Arribamax* was now blind, for without radar, radio, and their autopilot, all they could do was to keep their present heading, maintain slow speed, and track manually by GPS. Three additional lookouts arrived. The chief placed one on each side of the bridge, with the third assisting him straight ahead.

"Sir," interrupted the communications technician, "we've also lost our GPS tracker."

"What a nightmare we have at hand! Well, our compass is still working, and we have backup GPS units onboard. Chief, perhaps you can give him a hand with manual tracking, since it's not something he's had a lot of experience with."

"Right, Sir. Just yell if you need more help on the bridge."

At 20:55, Captain Jones shouted, "Chief, what was our last position relative to the Race Rocks, and our present heading?"

"The Race Rocks Lighthouse was three-three-zero at five kilometres ten minutes ago just before the radar and GPS went out, Sir. Our heading is still two-niner-zero, but we're bucking that wind and waves, and drifting to starboard."

"Great Scott! We could be in serious trouble. See if you can get some radio contact back." Calling the engine room, Jones yelled, "Lower forward speed to below five knots".

"We have one kilometre visibility now, but we'll keep the additional lookouts here on the bridge until we get through the strait."

It was now 21:00; they had turned northwest into the narrowest part of the Strait of Juan de Fuca 15 minutes before. They were now in heavy seas and storm force winds. Captain Jones picked up the ship broadcast microphone. "This is the Captain. We've just entered the Strait of Juan de Fuca and have hit unexpected high winds and seas. Anyone not on duty, remain in your bunks, and stay off all open decks, and keep open to this speaker for further instructions. Captain out."

Five minutes later, the wind dropped to 60 knots again, but with it, the fog closed in once more. Over the next ten minutes, as the wind decreased, visibility dropped under 100 metres, and by then there was no twilight left.

Despite their best efforts, the strong winds, fog, and loss of communications—combined with seemingly small human errors—all led to the *Arribamax's* veering to starboard, and towards Race Rocks southwest of Victoria. The captain and his lookouts were peering intently forward in the fog. The starboard lookout suddenly gasped, "There's a lighthouse starboard!"

Race Rocks lighthouse with shoals all around. Photo: Garry Fletcher, www.racerocks.ca.

The captain glanced to starboard and exclaimed, "My God! Race Rocks, hard a-port. Engine room, give us maximum speed now!" They all held their breath, but ten seconds later, the *Arribamax* lurched with a horrible-sounding scraping noise on the starboard side, and all hands pitched forward with the sudden slowdown. The scraping lasted for half a minute.

"Chief, go below decks and see what damage has occurred, and check on any crew injuries. We're already listing to starboard."

"Engine room, bridge here; report any damage please!"

"Captain, engine room here; we're taking on water fast. I don't think the pumps can handle it. We have a foot of water in the engine room and rising fast."

"Then stop engines and get your crew out of there, man. Get to the muster deck, and we'll decide soon if we have to abandon ship."

The chief was back in five minutes. "Captain, the lower deck is flooded, and there's no way to determine how bad the damage is. We were doing just over five knots when we struck those rocks, and the scraping lasted 30 seconds, so my estimate is that we've torn down 70-80 metres of the side of the ship. And we're leaking a tremendous amount of oil, so it broke through the double hull."

Captain Jones realized that there was no chance of saving the ship. He grabbed his microphone. "All personnel. This is Captain Jones. As I'm sure you've guessed, we've grounded out on rocks, the infamous Race Rocks, and our ship is badly damaged. We're taking on water and also leaking oil. Help your mates as necessary; I want all personnel at the muster station within five minutes. We have to abandon ship. We're in God's hands now."

Captain Jones then used their satellite phone to alert the Victoria rescue co-ordination centre of their situation, and that they were abandoning ship immediately.

To his chief mate, "Chief, go to the muster deck and organize the men, and get your second to do a roll call. It will be difficult getting everyone off safely, with the wind, fog, and oil on the water. However, the oil helps to keep wave action down. What we don't want is anyone jumping into the water in that oil and heavy sea. Let's have an orderly exit into the two lifeboats at the muster station. Our stern is in the lee of the wind, which helps us avoid the worst wind and sea conditions. You all know the emergency drills that we've practised onboard, so follow those procedures. We'll release EPIRBs from both lifeboats as we launch, so that the Victoria Rescue Co-ordination Centre can locate us if we get in further trouble. Above all, let's help each other and try to avoid anyone panicking. Get moving, then. I'll be along in a few minutes."

"Aye, Sir," the first mate replied, "I'll look after the crew, and don't delay yourself, Sir."

Arribamax struck the Race Rock shoals at 21:15. Twenty minutes later, the crew launched the two lifeboats and all crew abandoned safely, with 12 aboard the first, and ten, including the captain, chief mate, and communications officer aboard the second. Captain Jones used the lifeboat radio to alert authorities that all crew had escaped safely. Despite the high winds and seas, they made their way to Victoria harbour without further incident or assistance.

Then the real tragedy began.

With the high winds and wave action, there was little that could be done to salvage the ship or to stop the oil pollution. Before sunrise at 07:00 a.m., oil was drifting onshore at the Race Rock Lighthouse, at Metchosin, and along the beaches at Colwood. The shore all around Victoria and the San Juan and adjacent islands were now under threat.

Clean-up could not commence for three days because of the high winds, ensuring that this was a major environmental and economic disaster.

**

23. Disaster Aftermath

Carol arrived home from her night shift at 7:30 a.m. Eric was watching the drama unfold on TV. "Morning dear," Carol greeted.

"Mom, Mom," cried out Julia. "Have you heard about the tanker disaster last night?"

"Yes, I did. It kept your mother busy all night monitoring winds and talking with media." Then to Eric, "Very depressing, isn't it?"

"Yes, and I'm afraid our worst fears have occurred with this one," said Eric. "It was bound to happen, but at least no crew members were lost from the tanker."

"Dad, is this as bad as the *Exxon Valdez*? Remember the film we saw this summer."

"It might even be worse, because it's occurred near a populated area, with Victoria and all the Gulf Islands. And the oil spill will affect the fish and our orcas. Carol, have the winds died down enough that they can even attempt a cleanup yet?"

"They're getting ready, but winds are still gale force, and are forecast to persist for the next two to three days, because that low pressure system has stalled and is deepening along the Sunshine Coast. So there's very little they can do. Meanwhile, the winds, currents, and tides are spreading the oil much further afield. The *Arribamax* has broken up, and most of the oil has leaked out."

"It was carrying a full load, 100,000 metric tonnes, which is about 700,000 barrels of heavy oil. And experience says they can't clean up even 10 percent of an ocean oil spill. It could ruin our beaches for a long time. And since much of the heavy oil will sink with the weather delay, who knows what damage it will do to fisheries and tourism?"

***

Cleanup could not start for three days following the break-up and sinking of the *Arribamax*. By then it was too late to avoid the worst of the disaster. Despite past assurances by the federal and provincial governments, they could not organize fast enough to save the shorelines of southern Vancouver Island, and the southern Gulf islands of San Juan, Lopez, and several smaller islands. Environmental groups, First Nations bands, fisheries, and tourism concerns were demanding a full inquiry.

News media hounded and vilified Captain Jones, despite his being exonerated of any negligence several months later. That didn't help him much, for he suffered a complete nervous breakdown within two weeks of the calamity. No captain takes the loss of his ship easy.

Attempts to recoup costs of the cleanup and damage to fisheries and tourism were unsuccessful because of the Panamanian registry of the tanker, and court processes went on for years afterward. An immediate indefinite moratorium on all tanker traffic in the Straits of Juan de Fuca and Georgia were no consolation, despite pleas from Alberta to allow other tankers into Burnaby. The resulting furor brought about a first in Canadian history, in that both the federal and B.C. provincial governments fell to non-confidence votes by mid-October. The Alberta government fell in November as the Alberta public realized the magnitude of the disaster. For many Canadians, it had become an *inconvenient pipeline*.

***

On the Monday evening following the disaster, Eric went to address the Tsleil-Waututh First Nation in Burnaby, as he had agreed with Chief Curtis George back in July.

Both Carol and Julia accompanied Eric to Burnaby, given their individual interests, while John stayed with friends that evening.

Following a brief introduction by Chief George, Eric opened his talk with: "This evening I am heavy-hearted, as I know all of you are. What happened last week in the Strait of Juan de Fuca could have, and should have been avoided. The federal government had not paid enough attention to the advice of various environmental groups, First Nations concerns, and most public opinion in British Columbia. Cleanup operations are not going well, and experience tells us that ocean oil spill cleanups are rarely over 10 percent successful, anyway. This incident was compounded by high winds and fog for three days following the breakup of the *Arribamax*. But we have to expect such weather on our coastal regions, so no one can blame the weather. It remains to be seen how much this major oil spill will affect our West Coast fishery and tourism."

"I had promised Chief George back in July that I would give a presentation to you on climate change, then answer any questions you had about the science. I also hoped to provide more information on how we might convince government to withdraw some concessions given to Alberta and the oil industry. That information is useless at this moment, and I doubt that anyone is in any mood for the climate change lecture. Instead, Chief George and I decided to open up this meeting to concerns and questions from yourselves. At this point then, I invite anyone to come forward to the microphones in the aisles."

On the way home late that evening, Julia had many comments and questions, especially on the legal aspects of the disaster. Despite their sombre mood, Julia's interest in the disaster pleased Eric and Carol.

Later, Eric commented to Carol, "Seeing Julia's interest in this gives me great hope for the future. Our youth are concerned, especially where our generation has failed them on environmental issues."

***

24. Epilogue

By mid-October, attempts to clean up such a huge oil spill were deemed futile, despite federal assurances of hundreds of millions of dollars for that purpose. Most of 100,000 metric tons of oil were spilled. Powerful winds that had continued for several days following the *Arribamax* sinking, combined with the complex tides, had resulted in the spread of oil into Esquimalt and Victoria ports, and onto beaches of the San Juan and other Gulf Islands. By comparison, the *SS Arrow* that grounded out in Chedabucto Bay NS in February 1970 (shown below), spilled only 10,500 metric tons of Bunker-C oil, but the region remains devastated for fisheries and tourism today.

The Liberian-registered tanker Arrow ran aground in Chedabucto Bay, NS on Feb 04, 1970, spilling 10,500 metric tons of oil onto the water and beaches. 50 years later in 2020, oil remains on 300 km of shoreline. Photo provided by Glenbow Alberta Institute, Calgary. NOTE: The author was the on-site weather forecaster during the Arrow clean-up operation.

Heavy oil (diluted bitumen, or dilbit) initially floats on water, and much of it can be cleaned up at that point with 'booms' such as was used for the *Arrow* spill below. However, once exposed to the elements for several days, the mixture changes and the light and volatile condensate evaporates, while the remaining oil product sinks. Then it is very difficult to clean up from the ocean bottom. Here the oil had three days for this dilution to occur before cleanup could start, which was too late.

Oil pollution contained by boom from the sinking of SS Arrow in Chedabucto Bay NS, Feb. 1970 (Govt. of Canada archival photo).

The Canadian and U.S governments announced an immediate ban on fishing for the southern Strait of Juan de Fuca, Haro, and Rosario Straits, and surrounding waters south of the Strait of Georgia. The negative effects on fisheries and tourism for Victoria and the southern Gulf Islands were yet to come. They estimated economic losses to be well into the billions.

They declared the *Arribamax* spill at the Race Rocks an international catastrophe, and calls for reduced tanker traffic reverberated around the globe.

***

Meanwhile, the George family arrived at the Nicholson home on the Friday before Thanksgiving weekend in early October. Carol and Annie had planned to wrap up their book project, but the recent tanker sinking and oil spill gave them plenty more to add to their book, so they spent a few extra days.

Eric and Walter took the children on a tour of popular Vancouver attractions. On Monday, they attended a local Thanksgiving supper. The Georges headed back to Merritt on Wednesday morning. Carol and Annie planned to send their book to a publisher in November.

The Nicholsons drove to Kamloops in early December to attend Tom and Janine's wedding on December 10th. Jason had completed his fall exams the day before, and he was keen to continue with environmental studies.

Following the wedding, Tom and Janine headed to Hawaii for their honeymoon, while Jason accepted an invitation to go back with the Nicholsons for Christmas. Tom and Janine joined them in Vancouver on Christmas Eve.

Despite the environmental disaster, the Nicholsons, Beasleys, and Georges all ended the year on a cheerful note with optimism for the New Year. Julia and John were looking forward to their next summer vacation in the NWT. The Nicholsons had invited Leah Holmes, Julia's recent friend from Merritt, to accompany them, and her parents agreed.

***

Appendix - Main Characters

Julia Nicholson
  13-year-old daughter of Eric and Carol Nicholson.
John Nicholson
  9-year-old son of Eric and Carol Nicholson.
Dr. Eric Nicholson
  climate scientist, Climate Department, University of
  Vancouver (UVan), B.C. , expertise in climate modelling
  and impacts.
Carol Nichoson
  senior meteorologist/forecaster for Environment
  Canada in Vancouver, and Eric's spouse.
Buddy
  1-year-old golden retriever of the Nicholsons.
Wayne McTavish
  constable with RCMP Merritt Detachment.
Tom Beasley
  regional manager for Pacific Western Pipelines in
  Kamloops for the Kamloops-Nicola Valley areas.
Gramma Jane Osgoode
  former owner of Gramma Jane's Dog Rescue (ret.).
Walter and Annie George
  members of Coldwater First Nations band, owners of
  Horsekey Ranch, hunting guide, raise and board horses.
Jenny George
  10-year-old daughter of the Georges.
William George
  8-year-old son of the Georges.
Denny
  small terrier dog belonging to Jenny.
Arthur Green
  chairs a group from the Coldwater Fishers Society
  fighting corporate attempts to bar public access to lakes
  in south-central BC.
Jason Wells
  19-year-old son of Tom Beasley, having assumed his
  mother's maiden name.
Janine
  new friend of Tom Beasley.
Leah Holmes
  new Coldwater Band friend of Julia.

Jack Holmes
Leah's dad.
Chief Byron Tumelta
elected chief of the Nicola Tribal Association.
Chief Curtis George
elected chief of the coastal Tsleil-Waututh First Nation.
Captain Ross Jones
captain of the Arribamax oil tanker.

***

Abbreviations and Definitions

CPC   Canadian Petroleum Corporation

Cstbl   Constable (in the RCMP)

Emminent domain or Expropriation

> (France, Italy, Mexico, South Africa, Canada, Brazil, Portugal, Spain, Chile, Denmark, Sweden) is the power of a state, provincial, or national government to take private property for public use. However, this power can be legislatively delegated by the state to municipalities, government subdivisions, or even to private persons or corporations when they are authorized by the legislature to exercise the functions of public character.

EPIRB   Emergency Position Indicating Radio Beacon

IPCC   Intergovernmental Panel on Climate Change

MLA   Member of Legislative Assembly (provincial government)

MP   Member of Parliament (in the Canadian federal government)

PWP   Pacific Western Pipeline

RCMP   Royal Canadian Mounted Police

UVan   University of Vancouver

***

Author Biographical Sketch

Geoff Strong has had a varied career in atmospheric forecasting and research of thunderstorms, precipitation and evaporation processes, atmospheric water budgets, drought, climate cycles, and teaching the above. He continued his research into retirement during the early 2000s, but also took up the call to defend climate science.

While global warming and its cause from carbon emissions were universally accepted by scientists, climate denialists, funded heavily by the petroleum industry through third party think tanks, were using deceptive means to promote doubt and conspiracy theories concerning the science. The denialists use public and social media to spread misinformation rather than through refereed scientific literature. The denialists were successful because they were basically going unchallenged by climate scientists, most of whom rarely talk to the public.

With global carbon emissions unchecked and atmospheric carbon dioxide climbing rapidly, denialists represented a serious problem to mitigating global warming.

Geoff started giving invited public talks, simplified courses, and writing media articles on global warming. Always seeking novel ways to get the correct messages across, he even developed a bible study for the Anglican Church called *Questions of Environmental Stewardship Theology* (QuEST), which examines the problems of pollution and climate change with a scriptural context. More recently, he started writing novels and short stories on environmental issues. This novela is the third effort directed in this way.

Geoff holds MSc and PhD degrees in atmospheric science. He is a Fellow of and a former national President of the Canadian Meteorological and Oceanographic Society (CMOS, 2006-07), and has chaired a number CMOS centres across Canada where he has resided. He has received several CMOS awards for his work over many years. For leisure, Geoff enjoys nature walks with his wife and dogs, gardening, and is an avid reader. While writing novels, he remains involved in scientific studies of severe storms and of climate change.

***

If you enjoyed this novel...

If you enjoyed the adventures of the Nicholson family in this novel, then you may appreciate reading about their further exploits a dozen years later in *Convenient Mistruths*.

Canadian climate scientist Eric Nicholson, and his international colleagues, attempt to warn world governments about potential apocalyptic global warming brought on by methane release from melting northern permafrost and offshore methane clathrates.

Unprecedented severe storms were already occurring throughout the globe in response to the enhanced warming, while desertification of the African Sahel, with its itinerant severe droughts, had been ongoing for several decades.

A rogue international oil conglomerate is funding thugs to delay the release of the methane research, and they are prepared to use break-ins, sabotage, kidnapping, and murder. Meanwhile, Eric's daughter, Julia, conducting a survey on northern pipelines for her PhD in environmental law, collects data that confirms the methane threat. She becomes a prime target for the thugs. Will governments and people respond in time to avoid a tipping point in the climate, and global catastrophe never before experienced by mankind?

Available from the author or on-line at Amazon.ca or Amazon.com in print-on-demand or eBook format.